I0557728

The Long Journey Home

R. C. Smith

This book may not be reproduced without the express permission of the author. All rights reserved.

Any names, or characters portrayed have come from the imagination of the author, and not from real people.

U. S. copyright © 2018
All rights reserved
ISBN # 978-0-9983775-1-3

Other books by R. C. Smith

Thoughts Harrowing Edge
Gnarly
The Return of Mudge
Moose Trapped
Open Window Reflections in Poetry

Author photograph by
Jared Martin Photography

Book cover by
Up Productions

Dedication

For my horse friend Tuesday,
who became Sal in this story.

Authors note

Although this story was set in the 1800's, it is, in a small way, a reflection of my own life's journey.

I lived on a farm for a good while, and it changed my life. My experiences there helped to shape me into the man I am today. The horses and cattle I encountered over the years have left their mark on me. You may find their influence in my writing.

R.C. Smith

The Long Journey Home

Chapter 1

The Ohio winter of 1835 was an exceptionally harsh one, and Jess Fulmer had labored the previous spring, summer, and fall; preparing for the unrelenting cold that was presently upon the land. He had lain in a great store of food for the animals and for himself. All that could be done now was to wait out the long days of winter. Jess was quietly sitting at the hearth, absorbing its warmth while sipping some hot coffee. He had risen rather early this day, for there was much work to be done. Some of the cows had gotten out and wandered a good ways up Stone Hill Creek. This happened sometimes, and it was just one of those things that came with farming. The harsh winter weather was going to make his task much harder. He was reluctant to go outside, but he didn't have much choice. Jess had been watching the sky, and he sensed that there was yet another bout of severe weather coming on, so he decided to start rounding up the strays. It was daylight, and Jess had pulled on his warmest garments, shoved his feet into his boots and reluctantly went outside. He braced himself against the cold morning air and quickly ran over to the barn. The old Jersey cow began plaintively mooing, so Jess got the stool, the bucket, warmed his cold hands, and started milking.

    The sound of warm milk hitting the bottom of the bucket seemed loud in the quietness of the barn and the cow contentedly chewed her cud. When he had finished, Jess took the pail of milk to the house, came back to the barn and saddled the roan.

Jess lingered in the barn for a while, not wanting to brave the frigid temperatures. He stood and listened to the north wind howling, waiting for the sun to shine a little brighter. Jess stayed in the barn as long as long as he could and then finally mounted the horse and said, "Come on Sal, there is no time like the present. We might as well get this cold job done." Jess followed the meandering creek up towards the hills.

"Get up outa there, ya ornery piece of crow bait!" The mottled looking old steer stood its ground and refused to move. "It must be the cold," Jess thought. The low-lying wind was making the cold more intense. His feet were nearly frozen, but he couldn't see any sense in giving up at this point in the game. Cold or no cold the job had to be done. Jess longed for a cup of steaming hot coffee, but he put the thought aside and pursued the stubborn steer.

"Ok, you big old hunk of buzzard bait," he said. Jess's breath formed a white cloud of frosted air each time he spoke. "Its either going to be me or you, and you can bet your hide, it ain't gonna be me." Jess reached for his lariat and looped it over the reluctant cow's horns, cinched the loop and made the roan force the steer out of its hiding place. The angry steer fought against the lariat but reluctantly gave in to the horse's constant pull, and with a loud angry bellow; it charged up out of the draw. Sal deftly sidestepped the outraged steer. Jess deftly released the cagey animal as it went by.

"Good girl Sal, let's get this rangy critter's nose pointed toward home and get ourselves out of here." Jess pulled his hat a little closer to his ears and hunkered down against the intense cold. The leather accouterments of the horse made a rhythmic squeaking sound as he swayed in the saddle. Jess wanted to get home and about the only thing he could think of was the steaming hot coffee that was waiting.

In spite of the intense cold, Jess made it back to the cabin without any incidents and herded the cattle back into the corral. He was frozen, but that was just a part of winter on the farm. After dealing with the stray cattle he stripped the saddle off of Sal, rubbed her down, and then turned her into the stall and went inside for the coffee.

Jess sat in the rocker absorbing the heat from the hearth and watched as the flames cast dancing shadows around the living room. It reminded him of his loved ones who had once gathered there. He tried to put the memories out of his mind, but they lingered harsh in his thoughts and he began to relive those terrible days of sickness from three years ago. Jess was of a good English stock, and all of the work of farm labor had made him robust. Perhaps that is what saved him from the sickness. His mother had been the first one to succumb to the illness that fateful spring. It had been a hard thing to endure, but death hadn't stopped with his mother. He had helplessly watched as one by one his beloved family had been taken away. His father, brother and finally, his sweet little sister had gone by way of the grave. He had been left alone with no one to help him with his grief.

The neighbors on the surrounding farms came to his aid when they heard about his loss. They had helped him with the planting, and other chores that were too much for one person to do. Meals had been provided for a while, but when the days of mourning were over he had been left alone to make his own way.

That first year without his family had been difficult, but Jess had forced himself to stay busy. The worst time for him was always at the breakfast table. He had been used to the easy conversations with his family and it was always a harsh reminder of his loss.

At times the loneliness closed in on him and it became unbearable. When this happened, he would saddle his horse and go for a long ride; often camping out just to get away. It was a lonely life, but there wasn't much he could do about his circumstances so Jess kept working, just existing. All he really wanted was to have the closeness of family again.

Chapter two

It was around the end of March and Jess had been busy planting a corn crop. He had been working since daybreak and his back was sore. He looked at the sun to see what time it was and wasn't a bit surprised to find out that it was just nearing lunch time. Jess stopped planting, walked over to a shade tree and sat down to eat.

He began looking all around at what had been accomplished, but that didn't hold real satisfaction. He felt unfulfilled; frustrated by the emptiness inside.

Jess had tried seeking out companionship but for some reason, he just couldn't build a relationship with anyone. There were women that would have gladly married him, but Jess just didn't feel at ease around any of them. There were often times that he wanted to get away from all of the memories and start all over. But, because he felt a responsibility to what his family had built, he stayed; trying to carry on in the face of drudgery. Jess finished his lunch and cast all the troubling thoughts aside and went back to planting corn.

It was afternoon when Jess finally finished the day's planting. He rode back to the cabin, put the horse in the corral, looked in on the chickens, then went in the house to prepare supper before settling down for the evening.

Jess had been puttering around, putting things put back in their place when he heard the sound of a horse coming. He stepped outside in time to see a rather big gangly looking man just getting off of a sorrel. When he saw Jess, the man said in a deep kindly voice, "Howdy neighbor, I'm Bill Rolland. I was passing through and thought I would water my horse.

Jess replied, "Well, of course; come on in here. I'm Jess Fulmer, I'd be glad for the company. I've got some leftovers and you are welcome to them." The stranger thanked him and Jess showed him to the watering trough and gave the horse some hay to eat.

Bill answered, "I was beginning to run a little low on food and anything you have will be welcomed."

Jess invited him into the house and set about making a fresh pot of coffee and fixing Bill a plate.

Bill looked around the room and asked, "Son, do you live here all by yourself?" Jess replied that he did indeed live alone and told him about the loss of his family. "Well, from the looks of things, I'd say that you're doing a very good job of keeping this farm going, but say, don't you get lonely out here all by yourself?" Jess began to think that Bill was prying just a bit too much and didn't answer the question.

Bill saw the look on Jess's face and realized that he had hit a nerve. He said, "Son, I hope I didn't offend you by my questions. It's just that I have been on the trail for so long that I don't get to sit and talk all that much."

Jess smiled at him and said, "Oh, I'm not offended by the questions, it's just that I find myself missing my family every day. There is no replacing them. The two sat, sipping their coffee and when Bill finished his meal, Jess refilled his cup and asked, "Bill, where you are headed now?" He didn't give an answer right off, but hesitated as though musing over the question. He then replied, "Jess, I've been all over this I don't have anything holding me here, so I've about made up my mind to ride out there to see what I can see. I'm tired of this part of the country. I have great a yernin for something new."

Jess was being stirred by Bill's words, and began pondering upon them; he wondered if a change might be just the thing he needed. All that was really holding him to the farm was memories of his family and all that they had accomplished. Jess tried to put the thoughts aside and said that he hoped Bill would find what he was looking for and asked how long he was staying.

Bill looked around before answering the question, and when he did, he said, "Son you have a nice home here and if I hadn't been the type of man that just couldn't stay in one place, I could have had what you have, but I guess my lot in life is to wander. Oh, I sit still long enough to earn enough money to stake me, but then the itch to travel comes over me and I hit the trail. I was riding out when I stopped here, but I guess I'll be going on in the morning."

Jess offered to let him stay the night and Bill accepted, saying that he hadn't slept in a real bed for quite a while and that he usually slept on the ground, or even in a haystack sometimes. Jess was glad for the company and showed Bill a bedroom he could use and told him to make himself at home. Bill went outside and got his bed roll, turned his horse into the corral and settled in for the evening.

The two men went outside and sat on the porch, entering into easy conversation, with Bill telling Jess about his travels and of some of the bad scrapes he had gotten into. Jess listened with rapt attention, as Bill told of his adventures. The stories made Jess's life seem boring and wasted. He could feel the urge for a change coming over him, but resisted the feeling and put it out of his mind again. There was no use in getting his hopes up.

Jess and Bill sat out on the porch until the daylight began fading dim around them. The humming sound of many insects filled the air the soft croaking of frogs could be heard from the stream. It was a peaceful atmosphere that prevailed; so they stayed out on the porch until darkness settled in; then they went inside.

Jess lit candles, giving one to Bill, so they sat down at the table until it was time to turn in.

The next day Jess tended to the chores. He hadn't had breakfast as yet, but had put on some coffee, intending to cook breakfast as soon as it was daylight. Bill had risen also and was helping Jess with the chores in order to pay for the meal and the night's lodging. They worked until darkness faded before the sun's rays; then they went back to the house and Jess fixed their breakfast. They sat at the table enjoying the repast and when they had finished, Jess poured another cup of coffee, then went back outside and sat on the porch. Neither one of them said very much, for the morning was peaceful and they were quietly enjoying the sunrise. Then a rooster crowed, breaking the stillness. Bill said, "Well, Jess, sure do hate to leave such good company, but I guess I had better lite a shuck. It has been a pleasure getting to know you. Thanks for the hospitality my friend. Maybe our paths will cross again someday and then I can return the favor. I feel like I owe you."

Jess said, "Why, Bill, you don't owe me a thing. I've enjoyed your company. I needed to hear your stories. It helped me understand about my own situation. Now I have some deciding to do."

Before Bill left, Jess gave him a little extra food and some coffee. Bill thanked him again and then rode away.

Jess lingered on the porch a few moments and then, the loneliness came again. He tried hard to shake off the feeling, but it nagged him the rest of the day. Even though Bill was only an acquaintance, Jess felt like he had been abandoned. The conversations they had were still fresh on his mind and it set him to wondering what it would be like to get to see different places and meet other people. Then he began looking around at what he had, and put the notion of traveling out of his mind. He remembered the old saying that his dad always said. A rolling stone gathers no moss. Unlike Bill, he at least had a place to hang his hat. The only thing that was lacking in Jess's life was a companion. There were plenty of folks around that he could go visit when loneliness seemed overwhelming, but he still missed his family very much. Jess also knew that God was in control and when it was the right time, companionship would come.

All through the Spring Jess labored on. He had planted the garden, and by the end of June, the plants were out of the ground. The produce would be enough to get him through winter. His parents had taught him how to preserve the food and every time he snapped green beans, he would remember sitting out on the back porch, having easy conversations and he relished the memories.

As the long weeks continued, Jess began filling the storehouse for the coming cold days. At times, the drudgery of the work load got so bad that Jess had to stop what he was doing to seek a small reprieve. Sometimes, he would set the work aside and maybe get a book, go out onto the porch and start reading, just to have a distraction. If he didn't do this, the workload would overwhelm him. This made Jess think about selling the farm, but the load of responsibilities would always come back. It looked as if his destiny was to be tied to the land. If only he could understand. The loss of his beloved family didn't sense. His parents had worked so hard to clear the land and build a home, and now they were gone.

It was midsummer and Jess was cutting hay. He was swinging the scythe, taking wide swaths, trying to make as much headway as he could. At one point, Jess stopped to take a break, and he noticed that dark clouds were gathering. Jess tried to cut all the hay he could, for it had to dry out before putting it into the barn. Jess kept a close eye on the gathering clouds, trying to finish that section of the field before the rain hit. As he worked, the wind began to rise, bringing with it a cool touch of moisture. Jess paused a moment to watch the clouds. The storm was still a long way off, but there were flashes of lightning among the ominous dark clouds. He knew that his work in the hay field was over for the day. Jess shouldered his scythe and made his way back to the cabin.

As Jess walked through the hay, a wall of rain began forming far off in the distance; so he hastened toward the barn to get ahead it.

As Jess hurried, the breeze picked up and he felt the raindrops against his skin. There was only a smattering of them and they felt refreshing, but, with every step he took, they increased in volume. By the time that Jess got inside the barn, the rain came down in torrents. He stood in the door and watched as the storm's fury broke. It was fortunate that he decided to quit haying when he did, because the storm was one of those fierce lightning storm that often came upon them.

As Jess watched the storm unfolding, a great bolt of lightning flashed, lighting up the entire sky and the thunder rolled on and on.

It seemed that the storm would never let up. Jess watched the lightning striking trees and prayed that everything would be spared. He was very fortunate, in that the lightning only struck one rather large elm tree several yards away. Jess watched in amazement as the tree splintered and parts of it were strewn about the ground. The concussion from the strike and the claps of thunder that ensued shook the ground. Jess put his hands over his ears trying to protect them from the loud report and prayed for the storm to pass.

It didn't let up and he had to watch as the storm had its way with the land.

The wind blew leaves and small tree limbs around the yard and Jess had to shut the barn door to keep debris from blowing in. The thunder rolled and it became nerve racking.   Jess tried to calm the livestock, but the lightning and thunder made them nervous.

The Jersey cow mooed plaintively at each flash of lightning and loud report of thunder.

After having been trapped in the barn for an hour or so, Jess decided that enough was enough and made a mad dash for the cabin.

The ensuing result was that he got drenched and scared out of his wits by a close lighting strike. The ground shook and the thunder crashed as he jumped up on the porch and went into the cabin.

Jess, changed his soaking wet clothes, stirred up the fire in the hearth and put on a pot of coffee, for now he was chilled from the rain. He pulled up a chair close to a window and watched as the storm played out its fury; swaying the tops of the trees back and forth until the storm began to lesson and move out of the area.

Jess was glad to see that the storm was letting up; because there was still much that must be done. The episode with the thunder storm would probably put his hay cutting off for several days while everything dried out, but there was nothing else to be done. The weather was a very big factor and was one of those things that had to be worked around. Jess got out of the chair and poured himself another cup of coffee; its pleasant aroma and the warmth from the cup calmed his nerves. He went back to the chair again and sipped the coffee as he waited for the remnants of the storm to move out.

Jess was really growing weary of working the farm

and putting up with foul weather.

He hadn't really given himself any time to do something different. All of the hard work was getting monotonous. It was past time that he got away from the work, so Jess decided then and there, weather permitting, he was taking a holiday. The hay needed to dry out anyway and as long as the livestock had plenty of food and water, they would make it just fine.

Jess was glad he decided to take a day off and began making his preparations. He made up his bed roll and put some coffee and the coffee pot in a gunny sack along with the utensils. He would add the food stuffs the next morning. Jess began to feel better about his situation and the weariness subsided.   He looked forward to getting away, even if it was just for a day or two. He was learning that sometimes you just had to cheer yourself up when you were feeling down. It had helped him when Bill Rolland had stopped by. Bill's stories of the west had aroused his curiosity and once again caused him to wonder if he should seek another way of life. The farm was all he had known and he wasn't that sure if he wanted to risk losing everything, but still, the thought remained.

The next day Jess did the chores, making sure that everything was in order. He gave the cattle some hay and made certain that the chickens had water also. The chickens ran free and they would be okay.

Jess secured the cabin with a latch string, so the the wind wouldn't be able to blow the door open.   He gathered his belongings and waited for the sun to rise.

The morning was quiet and although there were some clouds gathering, this didn't bother him, he was determined to get away for a while and so started his trek.

Jess had gone across the field in back of the cabin and entered into the woods beyond.   He found a spot close to home but that was not what he intended; so, he went down a forested hill and up the other side. He walked at a leisurely pace among the oak and hickory trees. Jess didn't have a destination in mind; he wanted to hike, enjoying the day.

It was noon when a cool breeze arose. Jess looked up at the sky to see if any clouds were gathering, and sure enough they were, but he could tell that the clouds were only empty and there was no chance of rain.

Jess breathed deeply of the aroma of the forest and observed the beauty. Once he came to a small creek that had to be crossed. He deftly jumped from stone to stone until crossing safely to the opposite side.

Jess was really enjoying himself, reveling in the beauty of nature. He had hiked quite a distance and finally decided that it was high time he found a suitable place to camp. Jess cast around for a dry spot that had a small rise that drained well and it wasn't long before he was rewarded for his effort.

There was a clearing at the edge of some massive trees and there was an abundance of leaves and broken limbs strewn all around.

After stacking up the broken tree limbs he set about making a fire. First, Jess got some small twigs for the tinder, and found some dry moss in which to catch a spark from his flint. He placed some of the moss in the fire pit and it wasn't long before the moss began to burn; he then added a few twigs. As the fire grew, Jess put on larger pieces of wood until he had a fire large enough to cook on. The result was pleasing and soon Jess began feeling at ease and quietly settled down with a cup of coffee and began to relax.

After having found a nice suitable place to camp, Jess gathered up a few tree limbs with which to construct a shelter; it wasn't very long before he had a secure place in which to spend the night. Jess placed his necessities bag in the shelter, added some more fuel to the fire, sat back and began to enjoy his time away from the farm and all the work.

It was now about mid-day and Jess sat at the fire, and it wasn't long before Jess found himself getting sleepy. He resisted this, got out of the shelter and secured the fire. Jess walked away from the camp and went for a jaunt into a deeper part of the woods.

After traveling for an hour or so, he found a dim trail that went under overhanging tree limbs.   Jess began following this path to see where it might lead. He had never come across this particular trail before. It looked as if had been there for years and he reasoned that it was a deer path that he was following. Jess took his time, going at a leisurely pace; enjoying the scenery.

When he had gone about a mile or two he came upon a portion of the trail that dipped down into a rather steep brushy ravine. He stopped and studied the trail before following its winding decent.

About halfway down, Jess observed that a twig had been bent over. As he examined the area around it, he found a footprint. Jess tried to determine who might have made it. The longer he examined the more certain he was that it wasn't one of the settlers that had made it. Jess whispered to himself in an assured tone. "This footprint is a moccasin footprint." He began looking all around to see who was there. After some minutes he quit looking, knowing that if he were being watched, there wasn't anything he could do about.

Jess was curious about the footprint and would like to know whose it was. There had always been Indians in the area, but they had been looked upon as if they were only a part of the wild-life in the forest. Jess didn't linger at the spot any longer, but plunged ahead along the trail keeping an eye out for danger.

It was getting rather late in the afternoon and Jess wasn't sure if he could make it to camp before it got dark, and it was a strange place. He would rather keep following the dim track, but common sense prevailed and he turned around and went back to camp.

Jess had brought some bacon with him and so commenced cooking. The aroma of the fried bacon wafted its way up through the trees.

Jess had no qualms about camping alone and hadn't taken any precautions to conceal the fire; for he really felt it was unnecessary.
He had camped out many times before, and had never run into any real difficulty; this of course, was a little bit different. He had gone a lot deeper in the woods than usual and had gone into a part of the forest that he hadn't seen before and there was also the footprint to consider, but still, there was no real fear of his surroundings.

Jess was sitting by the fire, enjoying its warmth and tossing in twigs to keep the light going, flames and sparks lit up the surrounding forest. Jess reveled in the sight and sounds enjoying every moment. The aroma of wood smoke was tantalizing and the fire was making him sleepy. He didn't want to go to bed just yet, but rather, wanted to stay awake to observe the stars and perhaps the moon. Soon the light of the dusk faded into darkness. He put more firewood on and waited for the moon and the stars to appear.

It was quite late in the evening when Jess finally succumbed to the weariness. He had observed the moon and the stars when they came out, admiring them as they appeared a few at a time in the night sky. It had been a beautiful sight to behold and was well worth waiting for. But now he was tired and ready to turn in. Jess put the fire out, got into the shelter.

The next day, Jess woke up to the sound of bird song. It was a bright morning; he had slept longer than expected but he felt rested and was ready to go home.

When he got up, and looked around, and the first thing he noticed was that the camp fire was still burning. Jess was sure that he had put it out. This really bothered him, and the only thing that he could think of, was that somehow a spark remained and had caught the wood on fire, but how had the fire replenished itself? Jess began to puzzle over this, but couldn't come up with a plausible answer; until he came across footprints by the fire pit. Jess knelt down and began to closely examine them. At first he thought that it might be one of his footprints, but as he examined them he finally determined that they weren't his. Jess wanted to know who it was that had been there. He cast around looking for more clues, but didn't find a thing until he looked among the surrounding trees. There, behind one of the larger oaks, leaves had been disturbed. There were more footprints; they were like the ones at the fire-pit. The very thought that someone had been spying, made Jess angry. He tried to see if anyone was hiding, but no one was there. Jess finally made his way out of the forest.

Over the next days, Jess pondered upon the footprints he had found, but finally came to the conclusion that the prints could have come from an Indian, or someone passing through. It seemed odd to him, that whoever it was had started the fire again. Why would anyone do such a thing? In the end, Jess dismissed it and let it go. He didn't think that it was worth fretting over.

It was late in the summer, and Jess still had a lot of hard work to do. The garden had produced very well and he was gathering the last of the green beans.

As he went down a row he came across footprints in the moist soil. It was obvious that someone had been stealing some of his vegetables. He searched for some more footprints and was rewarded for his effort. Whoever it was hadn't bothered to conceal them, but had boldly entered the garden and took whatever they wanted. He began searching for more prints. He looked by the chicken house and found them there also. He went back to the cabin and retrieved his flintlock and proceeded to make a more thorough search. He found more footprints in the loose soil around the barn, then went inside and looked around. As Jess examined the barn, he found where someone had slept. It looked like Jess had an uninvited guest.

Jess went back to look at the footprints in the garden and examined them. He saw that they were moccasin prints. He began to think that they had been made by a stray Indian, or perhaps a colonist. He thought that the latter was more plausible, because the Indians had all been removed.

Over the next day or two the same thing was repeated. Jess became so frustrated that he went to the edge of the woods and yelled, "Listen, I don't know who you are, but if you want some food, just knock on my door and I'll give you food. He stood, listening, and waited for a while, but there was no response so he went to the cabin and started working again.

It was midday and Jess had been cutting firewood and putting it in the woodshed. The sweat was streaming down his face and he paused long enough to wipe it away. As Jess stood there admiring his work, he heard the chickens making a lot of racket. Jess ran to the other side of the cabin just in time to see a lone figure disappear into the chicken coop and emerge with one of the hens. It turned out to be an Indian. Jess didn't waste any time, apprehending him.

The ensuing scuffle didn't last very long, for Jess had thrown him to the ground.

Jess stood over his captive and could see that the Indian was rather scrawny and was probably in his teens. Instead of threatening him, Jess held his hand out to help him off the ground. The Indian still held the flapping chicken and refusing to let go. He tried to get away, but Jess grabbed his arm and held him tight. He was very surprised when the Indian spoke to him.

"Let go of me white man, or I will kill you.
The Indian had said this with vehemence.

Jess said, "Son, I don't think you're going to kill me. Now, let go of that chicken! I don't really want to get rough with you!"

The Indian began fighting, trying hard to escape, but Jess held on. Finally, after a few moments the Indian loosened his grip on the chicken and let it go. The hen cackled loudly and ran back into the chicken coop and out of harm's way. As Jess held onto the Indian he reasoned that the best thing to do was to just let him go, but instead he said. "You must be hungry or else you wouldn't be stealing from me. Would you like something to eat?" The Indian didn't reply at first. Then he proclaimed, "I am Grey Wolf, I am Shawnee. This land is my land and I will take what I need from it."

Jess was taken aback, for the Indians had been removed a long time ago.

He asked, "Has the proud Shawnee, taken to stealing food?"

Grey Wolf looked at Jess and replied, "My people have been taken, and I alone remain. The white man has stolen everything my people had. I will take whatever I want. It is mine!" Grey Wolf said this with such force and anger that Jess could not help but feel sorry for him. The Indians had indeed been removed from their lands, after that they had fought and lost the battle of fallen timbers.

Jess wasn't sure to about what he should do. If Grey Wolf was turned loose, he would just continue stealing, and if he stole from others, they might shoot him. It was obvious that he couldn't hold him captive, so he did the only thing that he could do. Jess let go of Grey Wolf's arms and braced himself.

Grey Wolf was very surprised when Jess released him, but he didn't run away. Instead he stood, as though contemplating. Jess took this opportunity to reach down and grab one of the chickens that happened by and urged Grey Wolf to take it. The Indian didn't quite know what to make of the offer.

He asked, "Why would you do this for me after I stole from you?"

Jess said, "You are hungry, and anyone who comes will not go away without food. Take the bird; you are welcome to it. But the next time don't steal from me. I will give you what you need." Grey Wolf hesitated, but it was offered it again, he took the chicken.

As the Indian left, Jess could see the pride in the way he walked.

Jess began to ponder on what had just transpired, and he realized things could have turned out very bad. Grey Wolf could have killed him. They had struggled together and when he had taken that chance of letting him go Grey Wolf might have struck him with his tomahawk, but he hadn't done that. When he had been released, Grey Wolf didn't even look back. It showed Jess that there must be good some in Grey Wolf and that if their paths crossed again, he might be able to help him.

In the following days, and as the summer turned to fall he wondered how the Indian was fairing. Jess hadn't seen a trace of him, and the thefts stopped.

Chapter 3

It was the first day of September, and as it often happens in the north, the days of fall brought cooler temperatures. Jess had cut all the firewood and stacked it for the coming of winter. There were still a few vegetables in the garden to be harvested, but, for the most part, gardening was finished. He had grown potatoes, and stored them in the wooden box in the root cellar along with some of the other produce. Jess had also butchered a large hog, curing the meat in the smoke house. It was just another one of the things he had learned from his dad. He still longed for his loved ones, but longing didn't change anything, so Jess plodded along doing the work, dealing with the loneliness as best he could.

On one very cold frosty morning, Jess was taking inventory of his food cash. He thought that some deer meet would be a nice addition to his larder, so, Jess decided to go hunting on the next day. He got his flintlock, powder horn, and ammunition pouch ready for the day's hunt. When all the preparations were complete, he set the gun and ammo aside and went about the rest of the day doing the chores until nightfall.

Jess, was sitting with his feet propped up on the hearth, thinking about the upcoming hunt; trying to decide where he wanted to go. After giving it much thought he chose to go to the area where he had gone camping. As he sat, his eyelids became heavy, and it wasn't long before he nodded off to sleep. Soon the gentle sounds of his snoring filled the cabin.

It was late when Jess woke up and found himself at the hearth. The fire had died down, and so he replenished the wood to make sure there were hot coals for the next morning. He went into his bedroom, laid down, and went back to asleep. Jess didn't wake up until a rooster started crowing.

The sun had just crested the horizon, and Jess was feeding the hogs. Their contented grunts filled the morning air as they ate their food. Jess had to stand back when he opened the door to the chicken coop. There was a sudden rush of feathers and loud cackles as the chickens emerged and began to forage.

When Jess got all of the chores done, he ate breakfast, got his gun and ammunition pouch, and made ready to go hunting.

He decided to ride his horse this morning; it would let him to venture a little bit deeper into the forest, and if he happened to shoot a deer, he could pack it out on the horse.

He saddled the roan, mounted, and started off, but the horse started bucking and almost threw him.

"Come on Sal. He said, what's gotten into you this morning?" Jess had to rein her in, making the animal go in a circle. This finally calmed her down, so Jess sat still and began talking to her until Sal was ready to go again. A cold wind was blowing, stirring the fallen leaves, but Jess didn't let this bother him and went into the woods, tethered the horse, and proceeded to hunt.

There was an abundance of deer sign, and Jess followed a trail they had made and took up a hidden position among a cluster of oaks; a few hundred yards away from the horse. There was a lot of mast on the ground, and he saw where the deer had been feeding.

The wind was still blowing, and it rattled the tree limbs, making it much harder to hear anything moving around. After waiting about an hour, Jess thought he heard an animal scratching around in the leaves. He focused on the sound until he had found its source. It wasn't a deer at all, but a big Tom turkey. He didn't really want to shoot it, so he watched as it foraged.

When the turkey left, Jess became much more alert. Redoubling his efforts, he moved farther into a denser part of the woods and concealed himself again.

By now the wind had died down making it easier to hear, and it wasn't very long before he heard some movement. As he watched, a rather large buck emerged from the brush and came his way. His heart began to race as the buck walked toward him. When the deer was within range, Jess took careful aim and fired. The buck jumped in the air, ran a few yards and collapsed on the ground, kicked its legs, and then lay still.   Jess didn't approach the deer right away; to be sure it was dead. He waited fifteen minutes and then he went to the deer. He poked it with a stick to make sure it was save to clean it.

The deer had been shot in the heart; and had died rather quickly, and had not suffered. If it had run off into the depths of the forest, he might never have found it at all. It was fortunate that it had been a clean kill. Jess left the deer where it lay, and went after his horse. It took him several minutes to get back to his deer and when he did, he found that someone had been there. Whoever it was had begun to dress out the deer for there were cuts in the hide. Jess looked around the forest, but there was no one to be seen. He had a feeling that he knew who it was. Jess dressed the deer, cut off a part of a haunch, and put it in the forks of a tree, then loaded the deer in front of the saddle, then mounted up.

Before leaving, he spoke in a loud voice, and said. "Grey Wolf, If that is you out there, I have put a cut of meat in the forks of a tree for you. If you run out of food, you are more than welcome to come and see me. I will help you." Jess sat for a few moments and looked around some more but knew that he wouldn't see Grey Wolf. Jess wished he would stop playing cat and mouse; if the Indian wasn't so proud.

Jess understood how Grey Wolf must feel after having lost everything. There had to be some bitterness in his heart; it must be hard for him to accept help from a white man. Jess lingered a little while and then rode home.

As Jess rode out the wind picked up, and a few drops of moisture touched his cheek. Jess knew that the weather could suddenly change, and if the temperature dropped very much it would start snowing. If it did, it was usually only a dusting, but it did signal the beginning of the harsh winter to come. The thought of the winter's cold spurred him on to cut more firewood for the long cold spell ahead.

When Jess reached the cabin, he started dressing the buck. When it was done, he built a fire for the smoke house and then hung the meat inside in order to cure it. As he worked, a few scattered snowflakes began to fall, the cold breeze swirling them around. Fortunately the snowfall wasn't great and after about an hour it stopped altogether. Jess rolled up the deer hide and soaked it water to soften it for curing. His wanted to make moccasins, and perhaps some leggings out of the hide. It was just one more skill his father had taught him, and it had come in handy.

Grey Wolf had observed Jess as he come into the forest, and watched as he hunted. He followed him at a distance, concealing himself in brush that grew in great profusion. He had seen when Jess shot the unsuspecting buck and when he left to retrieve his horse. Grey Wolf took advantage of Jess's absence to try and cut away some of the deer meat. Jess returned a little sooner than Grey Wolf expected, so he retreated and watched as Jess put the meat in the tree. He just couldn't understand why a white man would take his peoples home and then offer him food. When an enemy had been conquered, you didn't show compassion.

When he was sure that Jess was gone, Grey Wolf retrieved the deer meat and went to his crude shelter and began drying it. Grey Wolf thought Jess was a fool. The white man's way of doing things were so foreign. He didn't like the fact that Jess was trying to help, it rubbed against his pride. An Indian was self-sufficient; he didn't need help.

Grey Wolf tried hard to forget Jess. He wouldn't allow himself to give in to Jess's charity, but in the back of his mind he was thankful and couldn't get away from the fact that he had gone out of his way to help him. Grey Wolf tried to understand Jess's actions, and the stubbornness slowly waned. He realized that Jess's charity wasn't a trick, but that he was trying to help. He began to feel a kinship to him, and wanted to understand, to make sure his actions were really honest. Jess gave him food, so he decided to re repay Jess with his own offering of food.

A week went by before Grey Wolf caught two rabbits in snares. He dressed one rabbit for himself, but the other one he set aside. He made his way to his cabin, and. He observed when Jess went into the chicken coop to gather eggs, and then quickly came out of hiding, placed the rabbit by the cabin door and went back into hiding again.

When Jess came out of the chicken coop, he noticed an object by the cabin door. He picked up the rabbit and looked all around to see who had left it. Then he realized that it could only have been Grey Wolf. He held the rabbit aloft, and said, "Thank you Grey Wolf. I will have rabbit for my supper." Jess didn't think that Grey Wolf was ready to become friends; at least not yet, but giving him the rabbit was a good sign that the Indian was thankful for sharing the deer with him, and was finding out that not all white men were bad.

September was slipping away, and Jess gathered

the last of the corn and was bundling the corn stalks into shocks. As he piled the ears of dried corn in the wagon, he suddenly felt drops of cold moisture on his face. He looked skyward and noticed thick grey clouds gathering in. "I'm getting the rest of the crop in just in time. It looks like it could snow," he muttered to himself.

In that region of the Ohio valley, it often snowed in September. It was usually only a hint of things to come and Jess was grateful that his crops were in; because when it did start snowing, it would be in earnest with no let up. Sometimes the storms were so fierce that a rope had to be strung from the cabin to the barn so that he wouldn't lose his way in the blinding snow. He had heard of a family that had gotten snow bound, and one of them got lost in a white out and had frozen to death.

Jess hadn't seen anything of Grey Wolf, and wondered how the Indian was going to survive the winter. But then, he knew Grey Wolf was raised in the wild and understood the harsh reality of winter; still, it would be hard to survive the unforgiving cold to come.

Jess began to have greater concerns and wondered if he should look for him while he still could. As Jess loaded the last of the corn, a few snowflakes began swirling around him. He looked up at the sky again; the clouds looked dark and ominous. Jess knew that the first snow would only leave a few inches, but when the cold set in, more would follow. This prompted Jess to doing something, so he made up his mind to seek out Grey Wolf.

The following morning Jess got out of bed, and found that the temperature had dropped and that the fire had burned out. There were still some hot embers, so he hurriedly stirred them and added tinder. It wasn't long before he had a warm fire going, so he put a pot of coffee over the flames and began to cook.

After he had eaten, Jess looked outside to see how much it had snowed in the night.   It was still dark out, but the light from the cabin shone on the ground to reveal that there was only a dusting of snow.   He was glad to see it hadn't snowed much, because it would make the going much easier when he looked for Grey Wolf.

The dawn was rather dull, and as Jess left the cabin a slight breeze began blowing, and it made the day feel uncomfortably cold but, as the sun crested the horizon, he could tell the cold wouldn't linger long. Even though it was the last days of fall, there were bound to be days of warmth before the harsh finality of winter set it.

Jess did all the chores before looking for Grey Wolf, and it was around nine o'clock when he decided to saddle Sal and go on his search for him. The breeze had stopped blowing, and the atmosphere was warming up; there was a nip in the air, but it was proving to be a calm day for his adventure.

Jess had taken a lunch with him, because he planned on staying until he found Grey Wolf. Bringing his plan to fruition might prove difficult, but he felt that he had to at least give it a try.

Jess mounted up and made his way to the forest; frosted air rose up from the roan's nostrils every time that it exhaled its breath.   The accouterments of the horse pleasantly squeaked as they went. Its hooves made a hollow steady rhythmic sound on the half frozen ground; as Jess gently swayed in the saddle.

As Jess rode toward the woods, he began watching the sky above the treetops, hoping to see smoke from a fire. It would give him a better chance of locating Grey Wolf's camp. But, Jess could see no sign of a camp fire, but he continued searching. He examined the ground, but there weren't any footprints.

After following the trees along the field, Jess saw a

faint footprint in the dusting of snow in the shadow of one of the oaks. Jess studied it for some time trying to decide when it had been made and came to the conclusion that it must have been made early that morning, because it wasn't likely that Grey Wolf would be out and about before then. He stepped into the growth of trees to see if he could find the direction Grey Wolf had come from. He stood still and allowed his eyes to adjust to the dim light, and when he did so, a faint path among the trees came to light. Jess tethered Sal and began following the trail. It wound its way through the forest; until coming to a small stream that crossed the path. Here Jess halted and took up the search again; examining its banks. There was a stone in the middle of the stream, and on the surface of the stone was a clearly defined footprint. Jess was glad for this one footprint; for where there was one, there had to be others. He crossed the stream and began making a thorough search and it wasn't long before he was rewarded for the effort.

Jess had traveled perhaps a mile when he detected the faint smell of wood smoke. He halted and listened for any sounds, but there was none. All he could hear was the usual sounds of the forest. Birds were feeding on the ground, and an occasional squirrel could be seen jumping from tree to tree in search for its food. The place seemed to be devoid of human life, but Jess knew that Gray Wolf was around. He continued along the path through the trees until finding where the trail split and went uphill. He began following this new trail until he smelled the wood smoke again. Jess stopped, and after some searching, he finally found the camp.

The fire had been built under a growth of trees, and as the smoke ascended, the tree limbs caused the smoke to dissipate. It was a wonder Jess had located the camp at all. Grey Wolf' had taken great measures to conceal it. Jess looked around to see if he could find him but had no luck, so he boldly went on up the hill. As he examined the area, he found where Grey Wolf had been sleeping. Under a thick part of the trees, there was a hollowed out spot that had been filled with pine needles and leaves, and the only shelter above were the limbs of the trees.

After having seen this crude shelter, Jess was bound and determined to persuade Grey Wolf to stay with him throughout the winter. It would be to cruel to let him remain out of doors in the cold weather while he remained warm in his cabin, but persuading Grey Wolf to come in might not be so easy. The Indian was independent and not very trusting at all.

Jess wasn't sure of what he should do, and tried to think of a way to approach Grey Wolf with his offer. As near as he could tell, he wasn't around, but it was obvious that he had planned on staying, because of the great deal of firewood.

Jess finally decided to leave him a calling card. He left his foot prints around the camp fire and took some sticks and made an arrow pointing in the direction from which he had come; hoping that Grey Wolf would get the idea and come to the cabin. It was the only thing he could think to do, but with any luck, it might work. Jess took one last look around the camp and retraced his steps back along the winding path through the woods and to the tethered roan and left the forest. As he rode away he could only hope that Grey Wolf would to come to the cabin. Jess was sure he would understand the signs left behind, but there really wasn't much else he could do but to wait and see what would happen.

The reality of the winter came hard upon the land that year. Jess was snug and warm in the cabin, and as he went about his work; taking care of the animals his thought's often turned to Grey Wolf. He didn't see how the Indian could survive the winter.   He tried to dismiss Grey Wolf from his mind. There was enough to think about, and to do, without worrying over a stubborn Indian.

The snow, when it came, fell from overhanging clouds in great abundant flakes. It covered up the ground; piling up in mounds. There was a smattering of snow to begin with, and this storm added to the already bad conditions. The temperature was falling, and Jess was glad that he had gotten in plenty of firewood; for if the weather continued in this manner, it was going to be a long winter.

It wasn't that unusual for the "Ohio River Valley" to have strong snow storms, but this one seemed exceptionally bad. The snow started early that morning, and by nightfall it was two feet deep and there weren't signs of letting up. Jess had to care for the animals, and he struggled through the drifts to feed them. Fortunately, there was plenty of hay in the barn, but it was difficult to get them the water they needed. He had to get it from the well, and carry it to the barn. The wind was sharp and very cold, and each time he made a trip from the well to the barn, he thought he would freeze to death. It took him a while to do everything, and he was exhausted from fighting the cold.

Jess added more wood to the fire, and put on a pot of coffee, sat at the hearth, and listened to the wind moaning around about the cabin. The snow storm was still raging, and the drifts were getting much deeper. If the snow kept falling, he would have a hard time getting to the animals in the morning. The path he made to the barn had already drifted over, and if not for the ropes he could never have done the work.

This day, Jess thought of Grey Wolf, and hoped he would survive.   It was a shame he hadn't come in but he understood his doubt about trusting a white man. Jess hoped the bad weather would drive him in.

As the cold bitter days of winter continued to grip the land, and as the temperature fell, it became more and more difficult to manage the work load of the farm. Jess struggled to keep water for himself and the animals; it was a hard task that proved to be just about impossible. Jess was so weary of the winter cold. The ice and the snow had added to his burden, and he began to wish for spring. But in those climes, spring didn't fully come until late April, and sometimes into May. Winter was an arduous time of year, and there were times when it didn't look like it would ever be over; especially when cabin fever set in. Jess tried to busy himself with things to do, such as repairing the harnesses, or attempting to make a pie, but his baking attempts always failed. Sometimes Jess thought he was going crazy sitting in the cabin; with no one to talk to. When Jess had to tend to the animals, he spoke to them, just to hear his own voice; trying to stave off insanity.

It was late one evening, and the wind was howling. Jess had started cooking his supper when he heard some kind of a commotion. He looked out the window, to see what was going on. Jess saw someone trying to get into the chicken coop. It was bitter cold, and the person was having trouble getting the door open. Jess knew who it was; so he donned his coat, and went outside. Grey Wolf looked around when he heard Jess approach, and turned away from the coop and started to leave. Jess got there just in time to catch him. Grey Wolf tried to shove Jess away, but the Indian's strength was gone, sapped by the winter's cold. Jess held onto his arms and guided him into the cabin, and pushed him over to the warmth of the hearth. Grey Wolf was shivering all over, and held his hands to the fire, trying to get warm. Jess bade him set down in the rocker and then covered him with one of his mother's quilts and poured him a hot cup of coffee.

Jess felt sorry that the Indian hadn't come in. The blizzard would have made hunting next to impossible. There was no way Grey Wolf could have found food. The animals were holed up and not moving around. It was a wonder he had made it to the cabin at all. Indian or no Indian, this kind of cold was more than a match for anyone. Jess plated the food and presented it to him. Grey Wolf didn't hesitate, but hungrily ate.

After finishing, Grey Wolf sat where he was and looked around the cabin and decided that he didn't like the confinement. He put the quilt aside and then headed for the door. Jess didn't make a move to stop him, but, tried talking to him instead. He asked, "Grey Wolf, are you sure that you want to go back outside in the cold? You are welcome to stay here until this harsh weather changes."

Grey Wolf hesitated; as if trying to make up his mind and stood where he was, then finally turned and posed his own question.

"White man, why would you want to help me? We are enemies!" Jess wasn't surprised by Grey Wolf's question. After all, the Indians had been treated badly, as though they were inferior and the whites had run them off.

Jess weighed his words before replying to Grey Wolf's question. He wanted him to see that offering help was only his way of trying to show some kindness, and to see that most whites weren't bad. He began by asking, "Did you get enough to eat, and are you warm and rested? You are welcome to stay. The door is unlocked and you can come and go as you please, but it is cold. Why don't you stay a while longer? We will talk, and get to know one another."

Grey Wolf didn't quite know what to do next. His Indian pride told him to go out the door. Jess puzzled him, he had never been treated in this manner. The whites had, for the most part, treated his people with great disdain. He looked around once more, as if he was trying to decide. Jess remained silent, not wanting to seem pushy to Grey Wolf. He would have to decide for himself. If he left, he left. At least he had offered.

Grey Wolf, realizing that Jess wasn't out to do him any harm, and also because of the intense cold walked around the room picking up objects of interest to him. He didn't speak to Jess at first, not wanting to seem eager. His Indian pride was too strong for that, but after a while, he asked, "Why do you live here alone? Don't you have a squaw to take care of you?" Jess welcomed the question, and began to explain that sickness had taken his family away, and that he alone was left of his family. Jess told him that his situation was much like his. Both of their families were gone, and they had been left alone to fend for themselves.

Grey Wolf, although still a bit uncertain, listened to Jess. He began to comprehend the comparison, and understanding the constant loneliness that Jess felt. But he just couldn't grasp his compassion. A true warrior never showed compassion to an enemy, yet Jess offered to feed him after that he got caught stealing. Instead of striking him, Jess let him go. This had impressed Grey Wolf, and had caused him to consider Jess's actions, but he wasn't about to show any sign of weakness. It was something that had been engrained into his mind; it was a way of life to him and would be very hard to change. The longer Grey Wolf lingered inside, the more relaxed he became. It was warm, and there was also food and drink, and this helped to persuade him.

He said, "I won't stay, unless you let me work. "I will take no food unless you let me do this. I am a Shawnee; the son of a chief!"

Jess was relieved to hear this, because he feared if

Grey Wolf went back into the forest, he might find him dead in the spring, and what would be the sense in wasting a life because of stubborn pride? Jess nodded in agreement, and told Grey Wolf that his name was Jess, and reached out to shake his hand. Grey Wolf hesitated, then let his guard down and they shook hands in agreement.

Jess tried to make Grey Wolf familiar with his surroundings, showing him a bedroom, but Grey Wolf wouldn't sleep on the bed. He wanted to sleep on the floor by the hearth. Jess said he was welcome to sleep where he wanted too, and to make himself at home.

As the winter days advanced, Jess and Grey Wolf worked hard to keep the animals fed and watered. The cold was still very intense and they didn't think that the winter would break, but there were subtle signs of spring, and these signaled the end of the ice and snow.

It was the first week of March, and Jess had gone out to tend to the animals. In the distance he could hear geese. This brought a smile on his face; for with the return of the geese, Jess knew that spring was at hand.

Grey Wolf had risen quite early to check on some snares that he had set. Although it was still cold, the confines of the cabin had been getting to him; so he had gone to his old haunts in the forest. He had been living in the cabin long enough to become acclimated to Jess's ways. He came and went as he wished, but because of Jess's hospitality, Grey Wolf made sure to help with all the chores, and when possible, bring in some extra food; so on this day he had taken his bow and arrows had gone into the forest.

When Grey Wolf reached the tree line, he began casting around looking for deer sign. He was soon rewarded with the hoof prints of a deer. He didn't hesitate, but began to follow the trail. Grey Wolf very cautiously followed the animal, hoping to gain an advantage over it. As he studied the deer's tracks, it became apparent that it was the tracks of a doe; he broke off from following it, because it could be carrying a fawn, and he wouldn't take two lives, because it would be a great waste. He stepped off of the path and made his way to the snares.

Upon arriving at one of the snares, Grey Wolf saw a rabbit had been caught, and he quickly retrieved it and put it in his pouch, then reset the snare. He went on to the next one, and that snare had the remains of half a rabbit in it. He looked at the tracks in the snow, and saw that they had been made by a raccoon. He tossed the useless carcass into the brush, reset this snare and continued on to the next one. There was another rabbit caught, and he put it into the pouch with the other one and reset this trap also.

By now, the sun was well up; so, instead of going back to the confines of the cabin, he went deeper into the forest enjoying its quiet solitude, and again began hunting for a deer.

Grey Wolf went quietly through the trees and brush, being careful where he stepped. He made sure to keep himself concealed. The weather was changing, but the snow still lay thick on the ground, and there were a multitude of prints of the birds and animals that had come and gone. He paused to study them to see what kind of animals had been there; hoping to get a buck.

Grey Wolf slipped along from tree to tree examining the ground for tracks and was soon rewarded. There were fresh tracks of a large buck in the snow, so he very cautiously began to follow them.

The deer trail led deep into the dense trees, and Grew Wolf thought he knew where the buck would go. There was a large grove of oak and hickory trees not far distant, and he was sure that the buck would feed.

Instead of following the buck, Gray Wolf stopped and waited for it to get settled into a pattern of foraging. It took him a while to reach the stand of trees, but was soon rewarded for his patience. A large deer was feeding on mast, and when it raised its head to look around, he saw that it was the buck. He waited until the deer put its head down and then silently moved from cover to cover until well within range. The deer sensed that something wasn't right, and stood nervously looking around, but it couldn't detect any danger, and started to feed again. This was the moment Grey Wolf was waiting for. As soon as the buck lowered its head to feed, he let an arrow fly. The buck jumped high into the air, and began to run. Grey Wolf didn't pursue the injured deer, knowing it would run out of reach and he might never find it in the brush.

The buck had only gone hundred yards, and then stood very still; trembling. It didn't realize what had just happened, and it wasn't long before it bled out and collapsed on the ground. It kicked a few times then stopped breathing. Grey Wolf waited for about half an hour before going to the deer.

After having waited the allotted time, he followed the deer's blood trail. It wasn't long before he found the buck lying in a low place in a tangle of brush. He was pleased to see that the arrow had entered the buck's heart making a clean kill. He hoisted the deer on his shoulders, and began his trek back to the cabin.

Grey Wolf was made his way out of the woods, and constantly kept a wary eye out for danger. He had been seeing the tracks of a bear in the snow, and was quite concerned about it. A bear would attack a man if there was a fresh kill to be had. He was just moving under some low hanging tree limbs when he heard an animal growling. He looked to see if he could locate it, and it was almost too late; because a bear came charging out of the brush growling and snarling. Grey Wolf quickly dropped the deer, and began backing away. He knew that it wouldn't do any good to try and outrun the bear, or even to try and climb a tree, for the bear could easily climb up the tree. So, he did something that startled the animal. Grey Wolf stood his ground, raised his arms in the air and began yelling at it. The startled bear stopped in its tracks and began sniffing the air. It snarled at Grey Wolf a few times and then began backing away. It slowly turned around and then started lumbering off into the thicket from whence it came. Grey Wolf gave a sigh of relief and sat on a nearby log in order to catch his breath. It had been a close thing. He had come after a deer and rabbits, but had gotten more than he bargained for. But that was just the way of the wilderness. It was always out to get you. It could be a very dangerous place. Grey Wolf shouldered the buck, and made his way out of the woods.

Jess had been drawing some water when he looked up and saw Grey Wolf come into the clearing carrying a deer. When he got to the cabin, he tossed the deer on the ground, removed the rabbits from his pouch and held them up. Then Gray Wolf related his close encounter, and began dressing out the deer.

Chapter Four

The long cold days of winter finally began to change. There were still days of ice and snow that came and went; for winter lingered long and hard in Ohio. But, there finally came a day when all the birds that had flown south came back. It was a welcome sign that winter was about over. It wouldn't be long until the planting would begin, and the process would start all over.

Jess, was quite restless; the harsh winter weather had taken its toll on mind and body. He was getting tired of the struggle with the work load. Grey Wolf had been a welcome addition, but he knew that with the coming of warmer weather the Indian would probably move on. He had mentioned trying to find his family, and this had affected Jess. The farm, although it was his home, didn't really hold any real promise. The continuous work load was becoming drudgery and he often dreaded the thought of living just to be alone. There were several other families in the community, but they were spread out, and communication was lacking. He had, in the past, taken a day and ridden over to a distant farm and spent some time helping them with the work; just to have an excuse to break the cycle. There were single women his age and he had tried to get interested, but for some reason he just couldn't. He didn't know if this was because of the absence of his family, or what. It was just one of those things that he could not figure out, so he shouldered his loneliness and tried to accept his fate.
Jess turned his thoughts to seeking new places. Maybe he could make a fresh start. The more he thought about it, the more he began to desire change. He recalled the time that Bill Rolland had visited and how free he was.

he was.   Bill was like a tumble weed blown by the wind.

But at least he got to see lots of new country. His stories had stirred the longing inside of him. Jess began to want something different in his life, and so he finally decided to sell the farm.

When the ground finally thawed out, and the sun dried the soil; Jess plowed the field and started planting corn. It was an arduous process, and took many long hours. Grey Wolf had, as he expected, gone looking for his family. They had discussed his chances of finding them many times and Jess had tried to caution him about whom he interacted with, warning him to stay away from towns. Grey Wolf assured him that he would be very careful.

Grey Wolf had left early one morning at the end of March, and Jess had provided him with the provisions that were necessary. It was with a great feeling of sadness that He and Bill parted. Jess had become accustomed to him, and as Jess watched Grey Wolf walk away, the loneliness became more intense.

Jess had been putting off selling the farm until the crops were in. Now that Grey Wolf was gone; he didn't know how he could continue.   Jess also understood that he would have to plant the crops just in case the farm didn't sell.

Jess struggled along with the planting and all of the other chores that had to be done. It took him a very long time to get the seeds into the ground and he was becoming weary. His heart was no longer in his work, and the love of the family farm was diminishing. Then one day while he was in the forest chopping wood, he put the ax down, and proclaimed out loud. "I am sick of being alone! Oh God, will it all ways have to be this way? What did I do to deserve this kind of a life? Will I ever have a companion? Will my life always have to be nothing but drudgery?" Jess was so caught up in his sorrow that he hadn't even noticed that dark storm clouds had gathered. Suddenly a brilliant flash of light arched through the clouds, and a gust of wind arose; then there was a loud clap of thunder that echoed among the hills, shaking the ground. Jess was caught quite unaware, and he jumped at the loud report. He picked up his ax, and looked skyward. A very low dark cloud was descending upon him. The thunder had startled his horse, and it almost ran off with the cart. Jess clambered in, and started for the cabin trying to get ahead of the storm. The frightened horse swiftly raced across the field, bouncing the cart around leaving a trail of firewood in its wake. Jess tried to out run the storm but he didn't make it, and was caught in a deluge of rain mixed with hail. He tried to protect his head with his arms, but that didn't work. It was too difficult to drive the cart and dodge hail stones. He was still a ways from the cabin, and by the time he got there, he was soaking wet and quite sore from the hail strikes. He was fortunate in that the hail stones weren't large. If they had been bigger, he wouldn't have made it home. Jess unhitched the horse and led it into the barn, then quickly removed the trace chains and bridal, then turned the horse into a stall. Jess didn't even try to get to the house, but just stood away from the door and watched as the storm poured out its fury.

As Jess stood there, he began to think of what it would have done to the crops if they had already emerged from the ground. All of the hard labor would have been for nothing. The storm had added to his conviction that it was time to leave. Farming was in his blood, but all the hard work and the loneliness was overpowering him.

Over the next day's Jess struggled about leaving. His parents had worked so hard to provide a home.
It wouldn't be easy to leave.

He felt very depressed every time he thought of selling out. The farm was the only real connection with his family; there had to be another way to go forward. He wanted to leave, but also wanted to keep the farm. Jess was in a quandary.   Something had to give, so then and there, Jess decided to get more involved in the community. It was past time to set aside the death of his family and move on with his life. He made up his mind to start visiting the family that was closest to his own farm. They were the Springers, and he hoped that they would be a help to him.

When the storm had past, Jess emerged from the barn and took stock of things. There were a few tree limbs strewn about, and the chicken coop received a little bit of damage to the roof, but other than a good drenching, and a little bit of wind damage, everything seemed to be intact.

Jess picked up the broken tree limbs and set them aside to be cut up for kindling. Then he repaired the damaged roof on the chicken coop. It took him most of the day to retrieve the firewood that had been scattered all over the field. By the time that he got everything taken care of it was nearly dark.

April came and went, and the spring days turned into the warmer days of summer. Jess shouldered the work load, but there were so many times when it all seemed pointless. He didn't have anyone to share the fruit of his labor with. Then one day a traveling Parson stopped by. Jess had been putting up hay in the barn, and was just getting ready to go back out to the hay field when he saw a rider coming down the lane. He put his pitchfork down and went around to the front of the house to see who it was. As the man got closer, Jess saw that it was a circuit rider. There weren't any churches, and sometimes a circuit rider came by. It had been a long while since anyone had come through. Jess was really glad to see him come, for he needed someone to talk to.

When the circuit rider arrived, he stayed mounted and said. "Hello brother, I'm Parson Josiah Walsh. I have been ministering in your community and thought I would stop to visit with you. Have you got the time to spare?" Jess told him to get down off of his horse, and that he would put some coffee on, and round up something to eat.

Parson Walsh looked like he must be in his late-forties. He was rather lean and wiry, and his clean shaven thin face had a look of confidence about it. He got off of his horse, and hitched it to the rail in front of the cabin then waited to be invited in. As he waited, he observed that there didn't seem to be anyone around but Jess. The farm seemed to be very tidy with everything in place; yet he sensed a spirit of loneliness lingering near. Josiah set the feeling aside, waiting to get a little better sense of the situation.

After starting the coffee, Jess came out and introduced himself. "Hello Parson," he said. "I'm Jess Fulmer. So glad you stopped by. I don't get much company out this way. Come on in and sit a spell."

When Josiah entered the cabin, the sense of loneness seemed to be stronger. He began feeling rather sorry for Jess Fulmer, and then he realized that God had directed him to visit Jess Fulmer's farm for a reason. He patiently waited for the proper moment to minister to him. In the meantime he sat down at the kitchen table.

As the coffee made, Jess began making small talk, asking the Parson how many miles he had traveled, and how long he was going to be there. Parson Walsh began relating his travels. Jess offered to let him stay with him if he wanted to.

Parson Walsh thanked him and replied that he was very grateful for the offer; saying that he would be glad to have a roof over his head. For many times, he had to camp out. But most of the time he was invited to stay with someone. There had been many times that he slept in a barn, and once or twice, he had to sleep in a hay stack.

Jess related that the weather could be rather harsh, and that he had been caught in a hail storm, with no good place to go.

Jess was eager to hear more stories of his travels, and so he began to tell Jess about a curious fellow he had come upon not to many days ago. He had been riding along, when he came across a funny looking man that was wearing a pot on his head. The man wore a tow sack for a shirt, and he was barefooted. As it happened, they made camp together, and shared their food. The man's name was John Chapman, from Pennsylvania, and was selling, and planting apple seeds.

If he happened to find a good place for an orchard, he would stay until it was planted. From the account of John Chapman's travels, he had planted apple orchards everywhere, traversing a vast part of the country. Parson Walsh said he traveled with him, and even helped to establish an orchard.

Jess said that he would really like to meet John Chapman, for his life seemed to be an adventurous one. Parson Walsh realized that the stories he told were having an effect on Jess, and sensed that he was at an impasse in his life.

Parson Walsh could see who Jess Fulmer was. What he found, was a sensitive, caring individual. Jess had told him of the loss of his family, and related his desire for change, and of his wish to move on with his life. Parson Walsh was touched by the plight of Jess, and started ministering to him. "Jess, I have been away from my family for a while, and have traveled the length and breadth of the land. Everywhere I go, I find somewhere to lay my head, and I find food to eat. My journey has not been an easy one, but it is my calling. I have always found that God is always near at hand to sustain me when I am in need. There are times when I feel all alone. It is in those lonely times, that God's word comforts me, assuring me that he is near. I know that this has been a very difficult season of time for you, but if you will lean upon God, and trust him to help you, He will come to your aid. Now, as to selling the farm, and moving, I think you should reconsider. Just look at all of the sacrifices your parents made to build this home. Are you sure you want to give it up and walk away? If you will just be patient and wait on the Lord, he will give you your heart's desire. If I am any judge of character at all, I would say that you don't really want to give up everything your parents have built. It is just the loneliness speaking. I feel that there is something good in store for you, and it will come about in time. I do not say you shouldn't give yourself a reprieve. I just believe that you should keep the farm. Jess, all that I can do, is to give you my advice, and pray for God's will. You will have to make up your own mind as to what course to take."

Parson Walsh stayed on with Jess for a few days and helped him with the many chores that had to be done. Then one day he told Jess that it was time for him to go, but that he would be back to check up on him. Jess thanked him for all he had done, and that he would consider his advice.

When Parson Walsh rode back up the lane, the loneliness that had subsided returned again, and he thought of the Springer family. They lived on a nearby farm. They had children, and it would be good to go over. Parson Walsh had helped him come out of the self-pity, and he did not want to fall back into it.

Two weeks had passed before Jess finally found the time to go visit the Springer family.

He had managed to get a lot of fire wood in and also had hay put up for the winter. He didn't plan on staying with the Springer's, but everything was in good shape just in case.

It Saturday morning, and Jess had saddled the roan; she seemed glad to be away from the confines of the corral, and as they rode the up the long lane, her hooves kicked up small clouds of dust as she cantered along. Jess let the horse have its head from time to time to let it feed on grass; because there was no hurry, and Jess was enjoying himself. The strong smell of the horse, the squeaking of leather and the fresh morning air added to the joy of the ride. It felt so good to get away from the farm. Jess wished that he could do it more often. His morning ride was causing him to think long and hard about moving on, and so Jess began to focus on the beauty of the day instead.

It was about ten o'clock when Jess got to the Springer cabin. The first thing he did was ride Sal into a creek that was adjacent to the farm. She readily went into the stream of water to drink, and then Jess rode her out of the creek, dismounted, and walked to the house, tied Sal to the hitching rail and began to take the saddle off.

"Maw, we got us some company."
The front door flew open, and a young freckle faced boy with dark tussled hair came out on the porch and asked, "Ain't you Jess, from the next farm over?" About this time Mrs. Springer stepped out on the porch and said,

"Matthew, don't forget your manners boy. You invite Jess in!" Matthew sheepishly asked Jess if he would like for him to put his horse in the barn.

Jess smiled and said, "Yes, and would you mind giving her a good rub down? I gave her a good workout this morning."

44

Matthew grinned at the request and said, I'd be glad to, what is her name?"

"Her name is Sally, but I call her Sal."

Matthew replied, "Boy, she sure is a fine horse." He stepped down off of the porch, unhitched Sal from the hitching post and led her to the barn.

Mrs. Springer had been baking bread, and had her hair tied up in a scarf. She began to brush some of the flour off of her homespun dress; her face flushed a little as she tried to clean off the flour. She said, "Jess, forgive my appearance, its bread day, and I've got my hands full."

Jess replied, "Oh, don't think a thing of it. You remind me of my mother when she baked bread. It smells good; it's making my stomach growl." The aroma of fresh baked bread had wafted its way out side, and it was very tantalizing. Mrs. Springer invited Jess in and told him sit down at the kitchen table and rest awhile.

"Would you like a fresh slice of bread?" she asked.

Jess replied, "I haven't had a decent slice of bread for a very long time; that would be great."

"Okay, Jess, but you can stop calling me Mrs. Springer. Please call me Marta. We've been neighbors for a long time. Your parents used to come over, and pitch in to help with the crops. I remember this one time, when my Charles broke his arm. You and your dad came over and helped us put up the hay. So please call me Marta. How are you holding up Jess? It must be very lonely without your family."

"Well, Marta, It does get lonely. I try not to think about it. I'm doing okay, and have been able to take care of the farm. I have been getting my crops in and managed to put up the hay and firewood. Sometimes someone will drop by and help." Jess told her about Grey Wolf, and of Parson Walsh that had stayed with him for a time.

Marta replied, "We have had our hands full also trying to get everything done around here. Charles and Caleb are out on the back forty, raking hay, trying to put the last of it up before the weather changes on us. I'm so glad that you have had some help to get your own work done."

As Jess and Marta visited, the back door opened, and Abigail Springer stepped in. She looked much like her mother. Her long black hair hung around her shoulders, and she had freckles. Jess didn't recognize Abigail at first.

"Abigail," Marta said, "We have company. Jess has come for a visit."

Abigail, smiled, and said, "Glad to see you Jess. How are you doing?"

Jess had forgotten about Abigail, he was a little older than she was. The last time he had seen her, Abigail had been a young girl, but now she was tall and graceful.

"Oh, I'm pretty good Abigail. I don't have any trouble staying busy."

She lifted up the egg basket placed it on the counter and said, "Between the chickens, milking the cow, and the garden, it's about all I can do to get it all done," she laughed.

"I know what you mean; the work never stops does it?" The sound of their voices filled the room, causing Jess to think of the days when his family did the same thing. It gave Jess a warm feeling and made him wish those days could return. In a small way, they had returned.

Jess was glad he had gotten away for a while. Being in the presence of the Springer family had made him feel better.

Marta asked. "Jess would you like to stay for dinner?"

He replied, "Marta, that would be great. I haven't

had a home cooked meal in a while. Oh, I can cook some, but there is nothing like a woman's touch when it comes to food."

Jess couldn't stop looking at Abigail, and noticed how much she favored her mother. He was glad that he had been invited to stay. Jess hadn't even thought about Abigail. She was a bit younger than him, but Abigail had grown up. Jess began to feel a warm glow around his heart every time he looked at her. Abigail was beautiful.

Jesse's attraction to her hadn't been lost on Abigail, and she blushed each time he looked her way; she finally dismissed herself from the room saying she had a chore to take care of.

Marta sliced Jess a large piece of bread, and set a jar of blackberry jam on the table, and told him to help himself. The bread was still warm, and as Jess spooned on the jam, the aroma of the bread, and the flavor of the jam made his mouth water. "Marta, you are going to have to teach me to make bread, I can't bake like this. It's very delicious."

Marta said she would be glad to show him how. Then she asked, "Are you going to stay a while Jess?"

"I may try to stay for a month if you keep feeding me this bread and jam."

"Well, before you leave I'll give you the bread recipe. It isn't hard to make, and if you already do some baking, it won't be difficult to do. As a matter of fact, Abigail is really good at baking bread, I'm sure she would be glad to help you with it some time. Marta had noticed the look on Jess's face when he saw Abigail, and her woman's intuition told her that Jess was taking a liking to her. After having finished eating the bread and jam, said he had better check on his horse and to see if Matthew needed any help and went out to the barn. Matthew had removed the saddle and bridal, was giving Sal her rubdown.

When Matthew saw Jess come in he said, "Hi, Jess. I was just getting ready to turn Sal into the stall. She sure looks like a fine horse."

Jess replied, "Sal is a very good horse, I can ride her all day; she never bottoms out." Matthew finished rubbing Sal down, turned her into the stall, and forked in some hay.

As they left the barn, Jess asked Matthew if it was about time for his dad and brother to come in from the field.

"Well, he replied, they might not come in just yet. They are trying to finish the hayin. I'm sure they will be here before long. They aren't about to miss their lunch."

Jess and Matthew went back to the house to see if there was anything that needed to be done before lunch. Marta told Matthew to fetch more stove wood so she could continue baking bread.

Jess asked if there was anything he could do to help but Marta said, "No thanks Jess, just relax a while. Lunch will be ready soon."

Jess went on the porch, sat in the old rocking chair, and waited. He was so used to working that he felt a little uncomfortable sitting around. He didn't sit very long though, but got off of the porch and went out to the woodshed.

"Matthew, I can't set around. If it's okay with you, I'm going to split some firewood. I need to earn my keep around here if your mother is going to feed me dinner."

Matthew replied, "Help yourself Jess, we always need more firewood. That's that much more I won't have to split." Matthew took an armload of stove wood to the house, and Jess picked up the ax and began splitting up short pieces of log. The sound of the ax striking the wood rang through the air as Jess began to warm up to the task. Working for someone made him feel at home. It had been the right decision to visit the Springers. The loneliness wasn't as intense as it had been.

Jess continued splitting firewood until he heard the team and hay wagon pull up next to the barn. Jess sauntered over the wagon, and said, "Looks like you fellows have got your work cut out for you Charles."

"Hello, Jess. It's good to see you again. What brings you over here?"

"Oh, I had a hankerin for company so I thought that I would come over and see how you folks were getting along."

"Well, Jess, you came at the right time. Caleb and I are finishing the haying, trying to beat the weather. I don't want to leave any of the hay in the field. If it happens to rain, it would put us behind."

"I know what you mean; Jess replied, but I don't have as many animals as you do. I've already got my haying done, and put up for the winter. I had it made this year, there was a Shawnee Indian that stayed with me for a while, and then Parson Walsh came by and helped me. There is still a lot of work to be done, but nothing like there was."

Charles, was curious to learn about Grey Wolf and the Parson, and wanted to know all of the details; because news from outside the farm didn't come by very often. Jess told them about Grey Wolf, and Parson Walsh, mentioning that Grey Wolf had gone,
but that Parson Walsh was around somewhere, and that he wouldn't be a bit surprised if he showed up sometime.

Charles Springer brushed the loose pieces of hay out of his hair and beard. There were streaks of premature gray mixed in with his coal black hair, and sweat was running down the back of his neck, soaking his entire shirt. He stretched his long arms, and said, "Caleb, run over to the well, and fetch the dipper and water bucket. I'm parched." Caleb, who was the spitting image of his dad went to the well, and got the water bucket and dipper. They took turns drinking from the dipper, and then finished putting the load of hay up. Caleb watered the team, and led them to a shade tree, forked them some hay, and let them rest.

Abigail came out on the porch and said, "Dinner is on; better come and get it before it gets cold."

Marta and Abigail spooned out the stew, and then Charles said the blessing. As they ate, Charles began to relate what Jess had said about Grey Wolf, and that Parson Walsh had spent some time with him.

Marta, looked over at Abigail, and proclaimed. "Abigail, we had better clean up around here. This house is a mess. What if Parson Walsh drops by to visit?"

"Now Marta, you don't know that he will show up. Everything looks just fine."

"Yes, that's okay for you to say Charles, but I'm not taking any chances." She grinned at him and said, from now on take your boots off and leave them on the porch."

Abigail said, "And that goes for everyone else around this house."

"Caleb chimed in, "including you Abigail?"

Matthew started laughing and said that it was ok with him. "Now I don't have to bring in any stove wood. That suits me just fine."

His dad said," the chores don't stop. You can put the stove wood in a gunny sack and leave it on the porch." Everyone laughed at this light joke on Matthew, and they continued teasing him throughout the meal.

Jess was very glad he had decided to visit the Springers. It was good to be around a family atmosphere again. Of course it made him long for his own family, but it caused him to appreciate the time he had with them. It was going to be difficult to return home after his visit. It made him think that it was high time he started a family. He wondered about Abigail; she was pleasant, and good looking, but he didn't know her that well and besides, he was a bit older than she was. Courting had never really been on his mind after losing his family. But now, Jess was beginning to feel a change coming, and knew that he couldn't let things continue as they were. Getting away for a visit was just what he had needed. No longer would he let the loneliness overcome him. If he began to feel very bad, he would just go and visit.

It was late afternoon when the men came in with the last load of hay. Jess had gone with them to help get it done, and they finally finished putting the hay in the loft just about dusk, and in time for supper.

Charles remarked, "Jess, it looks like dark is about to catch up with you. Why don't you stay the night? We don't get much company."

Jess was happy to comply. "That would be great; I'd like that. Besides, it would be hard riding in the dark." They unhitched the horses. Caleb and Matthew, removed the tack, and watered the horses then put them in stalls.

When Jess and Charles stepped up onto the porch they were met by Abigail.
She said, "Please remove your boots guys, or there will be no supper!" They were a little startled, by the remark. They looked at one another and said in unison, "Yes ma'am!"

Abigail began to laugh and said, "thought we would forget didn't you?"

Charles and Jess smiled, removed their boots and then went into the house.

Charles said to them, "Well, you ladies think you have pulled one over on us don't you? Look at them Jess, they are having fun at our expense, that's okay we'll get our turn sooner or later."

Caleb and Matthew started coming in the house, but Charles said, "Boys, these women are on a big rampage. You had better remove your boots, or they say there won't be any supper tonight." Caleb and Matthew smiled, quickly removed them, and then sat down at the table and ate their supper.

When supper was finished, and the dishes put away, the family gathered together in the living room. The sun had gone down, and Charles built a fire in the hearth to add a little light and warmth to the room. The glow of the fire sent dancing shadows upon the walls; the ambiance of the room was peaceful after a long day of hard work, and they relaxed in
the pleasant atmosphere.

Marta got up and asked if anyone would like to have some bread and jam with some coffee. The men said they would like some. Matthew, on the other hand, replied that he wanted milk instead. Marta and Abigail went back into the kitchen to prepare the snack when someone knocked on the door. Charles got out of his rocker and went to see who it was. Framed in the doorway was a strange looking man. The light from the room fell upon his form. Charles was taken back by the stranger's appearance. He had a tin pot on his head, a gunny sack as a shirt and the man was also barefooted. He was an odd sight to behold. Everyone got up and gathered around the door to see who it was. They were surprised by the way he looked. The man just seemed to be a drifter, and they were a little doubtful of him.

Then the man said, "Howdy, my name is John Chapman. I'm just passing through, and I saw the light and wondered if I could spend the night in your barn." Charles remembered that John Chapman was known to be a funny sort of man, and that he planted apple trees. He didn't hesitate to invite him in.

Charles introduced him to everyone, and then they gathered around the hearth to get a closer look at this oh so curious individual.

As John Chapman entered the room, he said, "Dear Lord, please bless this home and all within," and then ensconced himself by the fire, stretching out his hands and feet to its warmth. Marta didn't hesitate but offered him something to eat, and also a cup of coffee to warm his insides.

John Chapman sat still for a few minutes, sipping the coffee and staring into the fire as though he were gathering his thoughts. He had taken the pot off his head and had laid it against the hearth. His brown hair was a little bit shaggy, and he had the stubble of a beard that gave him an unkempt appearance. But, his countenance was one of confidence, and when he finally began to speak, it was with clarity. He said, "I want to thank you for your kindness for letting a stranger come into your home. I have walked many miles today, and I'm gettin tired. I'm sure you are wondering what I am doing here today. Well, I am going through the country selling apple seeds, and planting orchards. I come from Pennsylvania, and I'm working my way through Ohio. I don't know how long I will be in this part of the country. I want to plant as many apple seeds as I can before winter sets in. If I don't get finished before winter, I'll go on back to Pennsylvania, get more seeds, and come back here in the spring. The weather is about to change and I won't have that much time to plant. I figure there are only just a few weeks of opportunity left."

Charles said, "I'm glad that you stopped by, we might be interested in having an apple orchard planted down by the creek. There is water year round, and the soil is rich. I think that it would be a good place to establish an orchard."

John Chapman replied, "if you could put me up, I'll

take a look at the spot, and see if it would be a suitable place."

Marta offered to get some quilts so he could sleep by the fire, but John Chapman said that he would rather sleep in the barn if that was okay. Marta reassured him that he was more than welcome to sleep by the hearth, but he said that the sweet smelling hay made a comfortable bed. John Chapman thanked them for their hospitality, bade them all good night and headed for the barn.

When he left, Matthew, who had listened to John Chapman's interesting story, spoke up and said, "Dad, he sure is a funny kind of man, ain't he? He didn't wear any shoes, and he had a pot on his head. Do you recon he lost his shoes somewhere?"

"Well, you don't wear shoes most of the time. I guess Mister Chapman just don't like to wear shoes either. Maybe he doesn't have anywhere else to put the pot, so he puts it on his head. Who knows for sure? Now, Matthew, I don't want you asking him any questions; he is our guest. As long as he is here you show him respect."

Matthew said that he wouldn't ask Mister Chapman any questions about the shoes and the pot.
He said, "He sure did look funny dressed like that.' Everyone laughed at this, and then began to get ready for bed.

Jess said that he would just bed down by the fire if that was okay, and that he would have to get back to the farm in the morning.

Marta told Abigail to fetch the quilts, and presently Abigail returned with them. She asked, "Jess, will you be okay sleeping on the floor?"

"Ain't much more different than camping out under the trees," he replied. I kinda like roughing it once in a while." Jess began to notice a nice quality about Abigail Springer. She had a quiet strength about her that appealed to him, and she was pleasant to look at and had also proved that she knew all about cooking. Abigail had many qualities about her that were needed for a companion. He watched her as she made his bed, and began to wish that he could get to know her better. But he didn't see that happening, for she seemed so much younger than him.

As Abigail finished making the bed, she stole glances at him too. She had noticed his strong features, and his very kind mannerisms, and also the willingness to work. This added to her admiration of him. Abigail felt sorry for Jess; because of the loss of his family. She knew that only a strong person would have stayed on the farm.

Jess and Abigail shared a few pleasantries after his pallet was made. Jess thanked her for the hospitality her family had offered him. Abigail replied, "That's quite alright Jess, I'm sure you would do the same for us too." She smiled, wished him a good night, and left the room.

Marta came in at that moment, and asked if there was anything he needed. Jess thanked her for putting him up.

He said, "Marta, I really needed some family time. You don't know how much I miss my folks. Thank you for taking me in today."

"Jess, "anytime you need company, just come on over here. Don't isolate yourself; you must have that connection with people. I know there must be times when you want to give up, but don't give in to the urge walk away. Just hold tight; I believe that God has better things in store, you just have to trust Him, and wait."

"Thank you Marta," but the waiting is very hard to do when you're alone." Marta smiled a knowing smile, for she had not missed the glances Abigail had made at Jess. Abigail was old enough to be thinking about a husband, and Marta saw Jess as a good match for her.

She said, "Tell you what Jess, I'll talk to Charles, and see if we can come over, and bring you a home-cooked meal sometime. I don't know how often we can do it, but it's the least we can do for a neighbor."

Jess thanked her for the generosity, and said he would look forward to the visit. Marta said goodnight, and went to bed. Jess stoked the fire in the hearth, added a little more firewood and lay down for the night.

Before Jess went to sleep, he could hear the subdued voices of Caleb and Matthew. He couldn't make out what they were saying, but he didn't really need to. The familiar sound of voices reminded him of his own family and he just listened to the pleasant murmuring, and drifted into a restful sleep.

Out in the barn, John Chapman lay curled up in the sweet smelling hay. He had used the sack of apple seeds a pillow and soon the sound of his gentle snoring drifted on the air. The horses had pricked up their ears, and snorted in protest, but they settled down.

The next morning, Jess lay still, listening to morning early morning sounds. A rooster had begun to crow; its raucous sound ringing loud and clear in the air. He got up off the floor, stirred the embers in the hearth, added a few sticks, and soon had a good fire going. It wasn't quite daylight yet, but Jess knew that Charles and Caleb were probably doing the chores. He got dressed, made his way outside, and went to the barn. Sure enough, Caleb was milking a cow, and Charles was forking hay to the animals. John Chapman was engaging in conversation with the men. He heard him saying, "Now if you have soil that is rich enough, I could start an orchard for you right away, and it really won't be too many years before your apple trees would produce. They would produce for a long time. to come It would be a nice legacy."

Charles responded with, "I see your point Mister Chapman. Why don't we take a look at the parcel of ground down by the creek after breakfast? You can give me your opinion, and we'll go from there."

John Chapman pondered a moment then said, "You know, I love planting apple seeds, building an orchard, just visiting with folks, making friends. But there is one thing I don't like. I don't like being called mister. My name is John Chapman; most everybody calls me Johnny, Johnny Appleseed. The name is fitting, so please call me Johnny."

Charles smiled at this statement, and said, "Okay, Johnny, we will." Jess joined in on the conversation for a few moments, and then if he could help with the chores.

By now, there were dim streaks of light in the sky, and Caleb said, "Its light enough to fetch some firewood; come on, you can help me if you want." They went to the woodshed and came out with armloads of firewood.

Presently Matthew come out of the house and went to the chicken coop. He stood back and opened the door. The chickens cackled loudly as they came rushing out, flying in all directions. Matthew had to jump out of their way, saying, you "crazy chickens!"

Caleb and Jess were watching this little drama unfold. Jess remarked, "Hey Matthew, did you just get attacked by a mob of hungry chickens?"

Caleb began laughing and said, "What's the matter Matthew, can't you control a few chickens?"

Matthew brushed feathers off his shoulder as he said, "Ahh, those crazy old chickens were just in big a hurry to get fed. I thought they were going to attack me" He started scattering feed to them, and they hungrily ate the kernels of corn, sounds. Mathew then went into the coop, and began gathering eggs.

Marta and Abigail had cooked breakfast, so Abigail came out on the porch, and looked for the men.

Jess and Caleb had finished the firewood and had gone back to the barn. She began to call, "Breakfast is on. Come and get it.

The men didn't waste any time going, but emerged from the barn and hurried on to the house. Jess remarked, "There is a real nip in the air, I hope bad weather doesn't come too early I'm not ready."

"Well, Charles asked, have you seen the wooly caterpillars? They have thick coats this year. You know what that means, lots of ice and snow."

The men went up on the porch, removed their soiled boots, and went in. The aroma of fresh coffee, sausage and eggs frying, wafted through the room. They hurriedly sat down at the table, and waited for their breakfast to be served.

Marta filled cups with steaming hot coffee, and Abigail set the food on. The women sat down as Charles prayed over the meal. There was a soft hum of conversation as they ate.

Jess looked around at everyone and was so very, pleased to be with this family. It was comforting to know that they were near.

Of course they could never replace his family, but it did help alleviate his loneliness.

After everyone had eaten, the men went outside while the women cleared the dishes. Charles asked Johnny Appleseed if he would like to look at the plot of ground for the apple orchard. He said, "If you want, we can hitch the team to the wagon, and ride down there, and if the soil is suitable enough, maybe we could start planting seeds."

Johnny Appleseed remarked, "I'm ready to look your ground over, and from what I've seen in Licking County, I would say that your soil will be rich enough to support an orchard. If your water source is good, is good, there won't be any problem planting the seeds. But we do have to get the seeds in the ground before the weather turns bad."

Charles told Matthew and Caleb to get the wagon ready. As they went out into the barn, Jess said that he would like to stay and watch for a while, but that he had better get back. Johnny Appleseed upon hearing this asked, "Son, when I'm finished here, would you like for me to come over and find a suitable plot of ground? I might not be in the area much longer. I have to get back to Pennsylvania; I'm getting a little low on seeds."

Jess whole heartedly agreed to this, and explained where his homestead was located. Johnny Appleseed said that he should be able to plant the orchard in a few days. It all depended on the condition of the soil, and if he had some help.

Matthew and Caleb after hitching up the horses, they drove the wagon to the house and picked up the men. When they arrived at the plot of ground Johnny Appleseed proclaimed, "We'll, you broke ground.
Charles replied, "The boys and I cleared this acre and a half last year, and had planned on planting corn but I think that an apple orchard would be just fine."

Johnny Appleseed began walking through the field, looking at the soil, sifting it with his long fingers. He remarked, "This field is going to support an apple orchard with no problem at all and you have already plowed it. That is going to make my job so much easier. With help, this orchard could be planted in short measure".

Charles said that the sooner they got to work on it, the better. Johnny Appleseed said that if Caleb and Matthew could be spared for a while, they could begin. Charles agreed to this, and said there were some other chores that had to be done, but that he could spare them.

Jess and Charles lingered in the field for a while longer watching Johnny Appleseed line out the ground for the orchard. He instructed Caleb and Matthew to make the rows just as straight as they could, and that he would go behind them and do the planting.

Charles said, "Johnny, I'm going back to the house, but when it is lunch time, I'll have the women bring it to you so you won't have to leave the work."

Johnny Appleseed replied, "That will work out just fine. There is much to do here, and we might as well work all we can today; you never know when the weather will change."

Jess and Charles, got into the wagon, and went back. Jess was glad he had decided to visit the Springers. It had restored his love for the farm.

Jess was saying goodbye to Marta and Abigail, and thanked them for the hospitality.

Abigail said, "Jess, we fixed a parcel of food for you to take home." She handed it to him, and as Marta patted him on the shoulder she said, "Jess, if it gets to lonely for you, don't hesitate to come over.
There is no sense in living that way when we are so near. I know that we can't replace your own family, but we will do everything that we can to help you."

Jess was touched by this sentiment, and thanked them, saying he hadn't had such a good time in a long while.

Charles said, "Jess, it was a great pleasure having you here with us, and if you ever just need someone to talk to, I'd be glad to listen. We will try to be here for you, it is something we should have been doing all along."

Jess felt better, and when he walked out the door, his step was a little lighter. He went out to the barn, saddled up Sal, and headed for home; knowing that everything was going to get better. Parson Walsh had been right when he advised not leaving the farm, the only link he had to his family. He now knew just how important the farm was. It might take him a while, but he wanted exactly what the Springers had, and believed that it would come about, but that he must be patient, and wait on God.

When Jess got home, he started looking for a suitable place to plant an apple orchard. He didn't want it too far away, and there was a small patch of land on the other side of the creek; after walking around on it, he decided to plow it up. If it wasn't suited for an apple orchard, another crop could be planted. Jess got the mule, and began to plow. There were big stumps and some rocks to work around, and those could be removed.

After about three days of hard work, Jess had the field just about ready for planting. He couldn't get one or two of the stumps out of the ground, so he set them on fire. First he got his dad's cross cut saw and cut notches in the stumps. Then he put in some hot coals. Smoke soon began curling skyward as the hot coals scorched the dry stumps causing them to burn. Jess had plowed all around the stumps, so that there wasn't any chance of catching anything else on fire. As he worked, he piled some dried tree limbs on top of the stumps hastening the burning. He had the two bonfires going and it wasn't long before the stumps were all but consumed. When the fire died down and cooled off it wouldn't be hard to remove what was left of them. All that needed to be done, was to dislodge the remaining rocks, and the field would be ready for planting.

When Jess finished working the field, he sat back and just looked all around him and began thinking about his dad. Everything he had been doing, he learned from him. "How could I have ever entertained the thought of leaving the farm?" he voiced. "My family is with me; every time I plow a field, my dad's hands are on the plow handles, and I can still see my older brother going out to the well for water. Whenever I gather some eggs or milk the cow, my mother and sister are still right here with me. I could never leave the farm." Jess continued his reverie, taking pleasure in the thoughts of his family; taking comfort in the fact that his loved ones would always be in his mind.

It was getting late in the day, and Jess unhitched the mule, saying, "Come on now Coolie, let's get something to eat." He led the mule into the barn, and turned it into the stall, and began forking in some hay.

He was just getting ready to exit the barn, when from somewhere outside, a voice called out.

"Glory be, you sure have done a good job on that there plot of ground, and its right next to the crick too." Jess stepped outside to see Johnny Appleseed standing in the yard. He was looking around grining from ear to ear. Johnny continued, "Jess, I been lookin at your soil, and it is as good as any I've seen. That there plot of ground is good for an orchard."

Jess, replied, "Johnny, I didn't even hear you come up, let's go in the house, and I'll warm some coffee, and we can talk about how many seeds need to be planted."

Johnny Appleseed looked around taking note that everything was in order, and not in disarray like he thought it would be. A man living alone often let things get quite untidy; he could easily see that Jess Fulmer had a well-ordered mind. He said, "Jess, you seem to be well fixed. You have a very good farm."

"Yes, my parents homesteaded this land. They worked very hard to make this place a home. I get lonely for them at times, and had thought about selling out and moving on, but I changed my mind about that. Where would I go? I don't think I could ever leave home."

"Jess, I pretty much live my life traveling all over, but that is how I make a living. My home is over in Pennsylvania. That is where I got my start. The farm is the heritage of your parents. Don't you dare sell your heritage it is the only connection you have with your family; you don't want to lose that." Johnny Appleseed's kind words encouraged Jess, and he knew that things would be much better in time, and that if he didn't isolate himself from people, he knew his situation would change.

Jess and Johnny Appleseed worked out the details of the apple orchard, concluding that a half acre of ground would be sufficient for his needs. They went back to the cabin for some supper and Jess said, "Johnny, I'll put a fresh pot of coffee on, and then fix us something to eat, then you can tell me what it is going to cost to plant the orchard. Jess was surprised by Johnny's answer.

"Jess, don't worry about the cost, I don't want money, I would rather barter instead. You let me stay until the orchard is planted, and share your food. If you have some cast off clothes to spare, that is all you need to pay."

Jess didn't hesitate with his answer, and said, "Johnny, that doesn't seem to be quite enough." But Johnny Appleseed assured him that it was more than sufficient for his needs.

"Jess, I feel that God has directed me to do this."

Jess really appreciated his kindness. It seemed like everyone he came across had been placed in his life to help and encourage him.

Chapter 5

It was now September, and all the crops had been harvested. The only thing that had to be done was to shuck all the field corn. Jess had watched it grow from the spring planting, and fortunately, the crop survived the storms. He had put the corn in a section of the barn that was out of the way for time being. He knew that the cold weather would be on him before long, so he decided to work with the corn on the next day, but before the end of the day, Caleb and Matthew Springer rode up. Caleb said, "Jess, we are going to have a shucking Bee at our place. There will be lots of food to eat, and a lot of fun. Have you shucked your corn yet?"

"Really, you are having a shucking Bee? That sounds like a wonderful idea. My corn is in the barn, and I haven't started shucking yet."

Caleb said, "We are getting the word out, and I'm sure that there will be plenty of folks that will show up".

Jess replied, "I wasn't looking forward to shucking the corn by myself anyway. I'll be glad for the change. It sounds like it is going to be a lot of fun. When is it?"

Matthew chimed in. "This weekend Jess, and I can hardly wait!"

Caleb said, "Jess, why don't we load the corn while we are here. It won't take us very long." Jess was glad for the offer. They hitched up the team, and loaded the corn.

Caleb and Matthew said they had another stop to make, so they mounted their horses and went their way.

Jess marveled at how things were going. Now there was going to be a shucking bee. "God sure has a marvelous way of working things out he thought."

It had been a very busy week for Jess, and the work load had been mounting as he prepared for winter. He had made progress, but what really made the week seem so long was that the shucking bee was Saturday, and he was getting anxious to go.

Jess had accomplished a lot in that week. The corn still needed husking, but other than that everything else had been done in time for winter. Of course there was always the milking to be done, along with all of the other daily chores of the farm, but that was just a fact of life that couldn't be ignored.

It was Friday evening, and Jess had put his tools away and was looking around at the farm. He began to think about his family, and as he pondered upon them he realized that he was becoming just like his dad. He even looked like his dad. His love and care for the farm had grown into him. The seed had been planted when he was a very young man, and now that seed had come to fruition.

Jess couldn't believe he had considered selling. What a mistake it would have been. His youthful urges had finally been set aside, and he was proud. All he needed now was someone with which to share his life.

It was Saturday, and Jess had risen early. The thought of the shucking bee had been in the forefront of his mind and he was looking forward to some fun that day.

As the morning progressed, Jess hurried, making sure the animals were well cared for. Then he cooked breakfast, hitched the team and prepared to go.

There was a decided nip in the air, so Jess waited for the sun to crest over the horizon. He poured another cup of coffee, sat by the hearth and absorbed some of the warmth.

As Jess sat sipping the coffee, the rays of the sun began penetrating the trees and filtered through the window.

He could see small dust particles floating around in the beam of light and thought that if his mother were there she would be dusting, making sure that the house was clean. He smiled at this, and then the sadness began to creep in again. Jess, rather than give in to the sadness, got up, grabbed his coat and hat, and went back outside and got in the wagon.

It was almost eight o'clock, and Jess had only gone about a mile or so, when a loud crunching noise came from one of the back wheels. Suddenly the wagon lurched to one side, and one of the back wheels came off. Jess hollered, "whoa, Bess, whoa Sam!" The wagon came to a halt, and Jess jumped to the ground and looked at the broken wheel. It wasn't broken, but had just come off of the hub. Jess looked around on the ground but the pin that held the wheel in place was lost.

The only thing to be done was to figure out how to get the wagon going again.

Jess got the ax out from under the wagon seat, went into the trees along the road way, selected a strait tree with enough girth to lift the heavy wagon and cut the tree down. He then gathered together some flat rocks with which to help lift the wagon off the ground.

Jess scotched the wheels, and attempted to lift the wagon. He had put some of rocks under the back axel and every time he lifted, he managed to place a rock on top of another until the wagon was off of the ground. He could only move it up a few inches because of the weight of the corn. Instead of trying to put the wheel back on, he tied a length of the tree up onto the axel and fastened it to the undercarriage of the wagon. It looked like a travois, but it held up the weight. He figured that if he went nice and easy he could make it back to the farm and fix the wheel. He got back on the wagon, and started for home.

Jess was making slow progress, and the travois jolted him around if it hit a bump.
He tried his best to steer around the worst of the bumps but he couldn't miss them all, so, he just continued on in this manner and tried to ignore the rough ride.

Jess had gotten only short distance, when he heard a wagon approaching. He stopped his advance down the road, and waited to see who was coming. Presently, a family from a neighboring farm pulled into view.

Jess recognized them as the Matthews family.

When the Matthews pulled alongside of Jess, Albert Matthews remarked, "Jess, it looks to me like are you are having some trouble. Can we lend you a hand?" He turned to his sons, Samuel and John and said, "Ok "boys, let's see if we can manage to get this wheel back on his wagon."

Jess thanked them and asked, "Are you folks going to the shucking bee too? That's where I was headed, until the wheel fell off."

"Yes, we are going." Mister Matthews said.

"Jess, "Mrs. Matthews chimed in, and I brought fried chicken and blackberry pies; we can't wait to get there!"

Jess retrieved the wagon wheel, and the men lifted the wagon up and Jess placed the wheel back on the hub. Mister Matthews had a spare pin, and he put it in place to secure the wheel. Jess unfastened the tree from the undercarriage and moved it out of the way. He thanked the Matthews for the help, got back into the wagon and continued on to the shucking bee without any more mishaps.

It was getting late morning when Jess and the Mathews family arrived at the Springer farm. Several other families there, but the festivities hadn't started as yet.

Jess parked the wagon and made room for the others in order make room for the shucking of the corn and attended to the horses, leading them to the water trough, then put them in the corral and proceeded to unload the corn.

By the time Jess unloaded the corn, everyone else had arrived and had gathered around the front porch. Jess sauntered over to the porch with the others and stood by the Mathew's.

Charles Springer stepped up on the porch, and thanked everyone for coming, and said that the festivities would start just as soon as the men and women were divided into teams, and reminded the young unmarried men that if a red ear of corn was found, that they could pick out a young unmarried woman and give her a kiss. This caused quite a stir among the young folk, and there were a lot of comments and laughter going on.

It didn't take long to divide everyone into teams. Jess found himself pared up with Samuel and John Matthews, Bill Wilson, and his two young girls, Sarah and Erica. They gathered around his wagon and waited for the shucking bee. Charles Springer then announced that there would be breaks from the work, with food and perhaps music.

After making his announcement, he said, "Okay everybody, now, get ready and lets start shucking some corn!"

At first there was a lot of calling back and forth, teasing each other as the groups began their work, but they soon settled down and focused on shucking the corn, trying to see who would finish first.

After shucking corn for two hours, Charles Springer stepped up on the porch again, and proclaimed that it was time for a break from the work.

Parson Walsh was at a table, and Jess hadn't even noticed that he was there. Charles said he wanted the

Parson to bless the food, and the festivities. Parson Walsh said that it was really great to see a community come together like this and have a time of fellowship and said that God was sure honor the gathering. He then prayed that each and everyone one would be blessed, and thanked the Lord for what had been provided.

When everyone went back to their places, they started shucking the corn again; Parson Walsh worked with different groups, spending time with each one, helping to shuck corn.

When he came to Jesse's group, he picked up an ear and started shucking. Parson Walsh worked quietly as if he were contemplating. Presently he sidled up to Jess and said, "Jess I would like to speak to you about something when we get another break." Jess nodded in agreement, and kept on shucking the corn.

The merriment became contagious, but Jess just couldn't get Parson Walsh's request out of his mind. He wondered what it was that he needed from him. Finally he was able to forget about it, because the next ear of corn he picked up was a red one. That meant that he could give any one of the girls a kiss. It was a tradition that had been handed down from generation to generation, and was just a part of the fun.

Jess held the large red ear of corn above his head for everyone to see. The young men around him began laughing and asking, "Hey Jess, who is going to be the lucky girl?
Pucker up butter cup!" Then they began to whistle and urge Jess on. He didn't really want to kiss a girl in front of the crowd but knew that if he didn't, they would tease him until he did. As he began looking around, Jess spotted Abigail Springer working with her mother. He held the red ear of corn and walked over

to where Abigail was standing.

When Abigail saw him coming, she leaned over to her mother and said.

"Mother", Jess is coming over here! What am I going to do about it?"

"Abigail, unless you just want to become the laughing-stock of the entire community, you had better kiss him."

Jess stood in front of Abigail, handed her the ear of corn and said, "Abigail Springer, I have come to claim my kiss."

Abigail gingerly took the red ear of corn and whispered, "Jess, I'll get you for this!"

Jess began grinning and said, "I will make this as painless as possible." He then took his hat off and used it as a shield so no one could see the kiss. Abigail blushed as Jess pressed his lips to hers, and gave her a quick kiss.

Someone called, "Hey there, what are you two younguns doing behind that hat?"

Everyone began to laugh at the fun, and patted Jess on the back as he returned to his wagon.

Abigail's heart fluttered from the warmth of Jess's kiss. she slipped the ear of corn into her apron pocket for a keepsake.

Abigail had enjoyed kissing Jess, in spite of all the whistling and the remarks that had been made. She couldn't help but like Jess, even though she didn't really know him that well.

After things settled down, everyone went back to the chore of shucking the corn. The varied groups worked for another two hours, and then break was called. They made their way to the tables and began partaking of the food and drink.

Parson Walsh told Jess that he would like to talk to him now. Jess replied that now was as good a time as any. They went over to a bench that had been placed in front of the barn and sat down.

At first Parson Walsh didn't say anything. He just seemed to be enjoying his food. But when he had finished, he said. "Jess, do you see that couple over there, the ones standing off to one side?"

Jess looked to where Parson Walsh was pointing and said, "Yes, I see them; are they from around here?   I don't recognize them."

Parson Walsh remarked that they were the Wilson family, and they were traveling on their way west, and had run into trouble. He said, "The poor folks fell in with some crooks, who robbed them of their money, and just about everything else; although they did leave them their team and wagon.

I have taken it upon myself to see if the folks in this community could help them out. They also have a young son; his name is Jiles David. Mister Wilson's name is Samuel, and his wife's name is Ruth.
Some of the folks have given what they can, but, they don't have a place to sleep. Most of the families around here don't have room. Oh, they could stay in different homes from time to time, but we don't know how long it is going to be before they get on their feet."

Jess realized where this was going, and broke in on him saying. "Wait a minute Parson. I know what you are going to ask of me. You want me to put them up because I live alone, and that I have plenty of room in my house. Isn't that right?"

Parson Walsh paused before answering. He didn't care for the tone of Jess's voice. But after hesitating he remarked, "Jess, I didn't mean to upset you. I know that your mind is still troubled over the loss of your family but there are times when we should reach out to others and set our own troubles aside. I just wanted to ask you to think about it, to see if you had it in your heart to help them.   It what should be done

Parson Walsh didn't even continue on with the conversation, knowing that Jess needed time to think.

Charles Springer got his fiddle and struck up a tune. As the sweet notes from the fiddle echoed in the air, someone started to sing.

Jess watched as some of the folks began to dance, swaying to the rhythmic tune. Soon laughter began filling the air as more couples joined in.

As Jess was watching, he saw the Wilson's dancing too. He wondered how they could be enjoying themselves after having lost all of their possessions. As soon as he had thought it, his conscience smote him and he began to rethink his answer to Parson Walsh. He said. "Parson, I have been thinking. I just watched the Wilsons dancing. They lost just about everything, and it reminded me of the loss of my family. The entire community came to my aid. I shouldn't have refused to help. I hope you will accept my apology."

Parson Walsh said, "Jess, I knew that you would reconsider; you are a very good man, and letting the Wilsons stay in your home will bring back the feel of having a family again. It will be a blessing. I'm sure, with your help, and of the community they will get on their feet again."

Jess asked, "Do you know exactly where they were headed?"

"Well, from what I understand, they were headed to Hope Well. Evidently they bought some land over there. Then he nudged Jess and said, "Isn't it customary that if a man kisses his girl he is supposed to ask her for a dance?" Then he looked at Jess and grinned.

Jess stammered, "Parson, I don't know anything about dancing; I'd trip and make a fool of myself."

Parson Walsh returned, "Jess, you'd make a fool of yourself if you didn't ask Abigail for a dance. Everyone kind of expects it. Besides, if you don't ask Abigail to dance, someone else is sure to."

Jess didn't hesitate a minute longer, but said, as he rose from the bench. "Parson, you sure do drive a hard bargain!" They laughed at this, and Jess made his way over to where Abigail stood.

As he approached, Abigail's heart skipped a beat. "I wonder if he is going to ask me to dance?" she thought.

Jess started the conversation by asking, "Abigail, are you having a good time? It sure has been a great cornhusking hasn't it?"

"Yes," she replied. "I see that you have a lot of corn that needs husking."

"Well," he said, it just takes a lot of effort, but, with all this help it will get done soon enough. I just hope the food holds out."

Jess took this opportunity to ask Abigail if she would like to dance. She replied, "I would love to dance with you Jess."

Jess smiled and said to her, "Abigail, You had better watch your toes, I am not much of a dancer." Abigail laughed, looked up at him and replied, "Jess, it looks like we are both beginners. Let's just watch. It can't be all that hard."

Jess and Abigail held hands and watched as the others danced. Abigail's mother walked over and began to encourage them to start dancing. They hesitated a moment longer, before starting.

Marta said, "Oh, come on don't be so afraid, you can do it. It's all just in fun. If you trip, don't stop; you'll get the hang of it." She gave them a shove, and Jess and Abigail moved into the crowd and tried to copy them. They struggled along, and just as they were getting the hang of it the music stopped and Charles Springer said, "It's time to go back to work."

Jess and Abigail lingered, then Jess looked into her

eyes and said, "Abigail, I really enjoyed the dance, even if it was only for a few minutes. Then he laughingly asked, "How are your toes?"

Abigail grinned and replied, "They're still intact. "Abigail squeezed his hands, gave him a big smile and went back to work.

The shucking bee went on for the better part of the day, and about supper time, the Matthews team finished shucking their corn. They gave a loud shout and Mister Matthews climbed up on to the front of his wagon and said, "I don't believe I've ever seen such slow people before. Are we going to have to help everyone else finish?" Then Charles Springer said that he would let them shuck his load of corn any time.

The Matthews's got refreshment, and built up the fire, for it had gotten cooler, and it wasn't long before Charles Springer got his fiddle and struck up a familiar fiddle tune, and the sweet mellow notes of music began rising in the cool fall air.

Parson Walsh began singing the song, and soon the others joined in, and their melodic voices drifted far over the hills.

Jess stood still, listening. Then his family came to mind, and the sadness that had been put aside, came rushing in. He felt very much alone, even in the crowd of friends.

As Jess thought about his family, he realized that perhaps the Wilsons were a part of the answer to his loneliness. If they stayed with him things could get a little better; it would help bring back some of what he had lost.

Jess didn't wait for Parson Walsh to remind him about the Wilsons. He made his way over to them and introduces himself. Mister Wilson was getting a plate of food, and when he had finished, Jess said, "Hi, I'm Jess Fulmer, and I have a farm about five miles from here. Have you been enjoying the husking bee?"

"I'm Glad to meet you Jess, I'm Samuel Wilson, this is Ruth, and this is our son Jiles David. We were passing through on our way to Hope Well when we had a run in with some rough necks who robbed us. They got away with about everything that we owned. There is no telling how long it will be before we hear anything from our folks. We had sold our place back East, and were going to start over out here. But, as you can see, we have nowhere to go. These kind folks are going to put us up for a few days until we can decide what to do."

Jess had quietly listened to this narrative, and when Samuel Wilson had finished talking he said, "Mister Wilson, you know, my family died a few years ago, and I live alone. I have lots of room, so, instead of staying with the Springers or anyone else, why don't you and your family stay with me until you get things sorted out? "Think it over, and let me know what you want to do."

They thanked Jess for the kind offer, and said that they would think it over.

Jess didn't blame them for not answering him right away, they had been through a lot of trouble, and just wanted to be sure that it was okay. Jess wandered around offering to help anyone that needed a hand. He finally ended up at his wagon. He started to shuck the remaining corn when he saw Albert Matthews coming.

"Well Jess, he asked, did you have a good time?"

"Yes I did; it was a lot fun. I needed the break from all of the farm work.

Albert and Jess began shoveling all of the shucked corn into the wagon, and it wasn't long before the job was done and everyone began to gather around the tables again. The women had prepared some more food and soon everyone began eating the meal. The men had added fuel to the fire, and it wasn't long until folks began drifting to its warmth, because the wind had picked up, and there was the smell of rain in the air. Soon, dark clouds formed, and the pungent aroma of the rain became stronger. The men rushed to the wagons to cover the corn, while the women covered the tables.

Presently a few drops of rain descended, but the merry makers ignored this, and went back to the fire, but the rain started pouring down. Everyone tried to run away from the downpour. The women ran to the Springer's house, while the men ran into the barn, and gathered at the door and watched the rain storm.

It began to lightning, with loud booms of thunder, but the storm soon moved out, of the area leaving everything drenched.

With the passing of the thunderstorm, everyone gathered their belongings, and got ready to go to their homes. Parson Walsh had been staying at the Springers home while he ministered to the needs of the community, but now felt that it was time to move on. His circuit took several months to make, and it would be some time before he returned. He was making his rounds saying his goodbyes before leaving. When he came to Jess, he said,   "Brother Jess, I am proud that you are helping the Wilsons; it was the right thing."

Jess replied, "Parson, the more I thought about it, the more I began to think about my own situation and how they must miss their families. It is not a good feeling. I need to do my part to help them get on with their lives. They can stay for as long as it takes."

Parson Walsh assured him that they were good people; he didn't think that they would be staying that long; probably until their folks back east sent them some money. Jess said it would all be okay if they worked together.

The festivities had been dampened by the rain, but

the corn had been husked, so each family began making their way home.

Jess was helping Samuel Wilson, with his team and wagon while Ruth and Jiles David said their goodbyes. When they returned to the wagon, Jess and Samuel had everything ready to go. Ruth said to Jess, "We are very grateful to you for taking us in. I don't know how we can ever repay you."

Jess said, "I'm glad I could help you out, and I'm sure things will turn around for you." Jess set his doubts aside, and was committed to go through with letting the Wilsons stay.

Ruth had detected a slight hesitation in his voice, but said nothing; she was just glad that they would have a roof over their heads.

Before Jess left, he thanked the Springers for inviting him to the husking bee. Charles said, "Jess, if you need help of any kind, just let me know, I'll be glad to lend a hand. What you are doing for the Wilsons is a good thing, and I'm sure they are going help you with the work around the farm. If things get a little crowded for you, come on over and you can have a meal with us some time."

Jess thanked Charles, and said, "No doubt about it Charles, I will need breathing room sometimes." They laughed at this and Marta and Abigail, who had been listening to their conversation, told Jess they expected him to drop by.

As Jess started to leave, Abigail followed him out onto the porch, and thanked him for the dance they had. She was looking up at him smiling. Jess smiled back at her and said, "Abigail, thank you for being kind. I felt right at home."

"Jess", she said, "we meant it when we said that you are welcome to come back any time." When Abigail said this, she touched his shirt sleeve. Jess just stood there, unsure of what to do next. Abigail looked him in the eyes, as if waiting for a response. Jess cleared his throat, and said, "Well, Abigail, I most certainly will come back. Your family has been very good to me, and your cooking is so much better than mine." They laughed about his comment, and then Jess said that he had better get going before it got too dark.

Abigail stayed on the porch watching him; she wondered if Jess really would come back.

After the Matthews started for home, Jess turned his team behind them and the Wilsons followed. It was getting very near dark, and there was still a mile or so to go before they got home, so Jess said that they had better stop long enough to light a lantern. Jess took this opportunity to ask if Jiles David would like to ride in his wagon with him. Jiles David said he would like that very much, and his mother told him to go ahead, but to behave and to do as he was told. Jiles jumped from their wagon and climbed up beside Jess.

The lantern didn't give off much light, but it was enough. The soft glow from the lantern cast dim shadows as they went along. It was getting late when the travelers got home, and they were weary from the days events. The horses were unhitched and turned into the corral. Then Jess invited the Wilsons into his home.

He went into the house and began lighting lanterns. As near as he could tell, everything was undisturbed. He built a fire in the hearth, and showed the Wilsons around. Ruth went straight to the hearth and began warming her hands. She looked around at the furnishings, admiring the craftsmanship. It was obvious to Ruth that someone had taken care in building of this home.

Samuel came in, and remarked, "Ruth, we are very fortunate to have been taken in by Jess."

"Yes indeed," "I don't know what would have done

if we hadn't come to this community of fine folks."

Jess showed Jiles David a small room and said, "Jiles, this was my little sister's room. You are welcome to use it if your mom and dad says it is okay. Why don't you ask them if you can sleep here?"

Jiles looked at the room, then sat on the bed, and commented, "Jess, this bed is sure softer than that old wagon. I'd like sleeping in here. I'll go ask if I can."

Jiles went into the living room and looked up at his dad and said, "Dad, there is a nice soft bed in that room. Jess said I could sleep in there if you said it was okay.   I shore am tired of sleeping in that old wagon. Can I"?

Samuel replied, "Well, Jiles David, as long as Jess doesn't mind. I'm tired of sleeping in that old wagon myself." Jiles David went back into the bedroom and began bouncing up and down on the bed, testing its softness.

After a few moments his mother came in. Jiles David had fallen fast asleep. She stood looking around at the nice room, and tears began welling up in her eyes. When they had been robbed, she thought that their dream of going west to start a new home was over. Now as she looked down at her sleeping child in a stranger's house, new hope began to arise. They were safe; thanks to a stranger's kindness. Everything that had happened since the robbery had been a God send, and she was very thankful. Ruth went out of the room, got a lantern, went outside, and began bringing in some clothing. She went back in and got Jiles David dressed for bed and tucked him in. Jess had made a pot of coffee, and was hanging it on one of the hooks at the hearth when Ruth came into the room. She asked, "Jess, is there anything that we can do? We are so grateful that you took us in. How we can ever repay you."

"Well Ruth, I'm very sure that if I needed a place

to stay that you would help me out too. Tell you what, tomorrow, you can fix breakfast. I can cook some, but I sure miss biscuits with my breakfast.   The ones I try to make turn out hard as rocks!" Ruth laughed, and promised that she would make a pan full in the morning.

Samuel had been outside, and brought in a trunk of clothes and asked Jess where they should sleep.

Jess said, "Samuel, you and Ruth stay in my parent's bedroom. I'll sleep in my room; it's what I am used to."

Samuel protested, replying, "Jess, I don't think that it would be right to take the best room in the house. We just wouldn't feel right about it."

"I don't go into my parent's room often Samuel and it would be good to have it occupied again. I know they would want you to use their room; you are welcome to it."

Ruth said,   "Jess, this is very kind of you. It sure will feel good to sleep in a bed again, and have a roof over our heads."

The coffee was made, so Jess got some cups and they went to the hearth to drink the coffee.   The Wilsons were still overcome with his hospitality, and thanked Jess once more, for what he had done for them.

Samuel said, "Jess, you have been a God send. Ruth and I were talking a while ago, and could see how God used you to deliver us. I don't know how we can ever repay you for your kindness."

"Samuel, it was the Christian thing to do. This is a good community, and any one would have done the same.   There is plenty of work to do, and you won't have to feel obligated, if you can help me with the chores.

"Something sure does smell good. Mom must be cooking my breakfast."

Jess was stirring awake. The faint image of his mother lingered in his mind, and he reluctantly got out of bed.

Jess knew that it was Ruth cooking breakfast. The sound and smell of the bacon, was quite tantalizing.

Ruth had biscuits in the oven that were about ready to come out, and they smelled wonderful. "Ruth, I haven't smelled biscuits so heavenly for a very long time."

Samuel, had just come in, he said, "Jess, let me tell you all about my Ruth. She is an excellent cook, her mother taught her well. It's a wonder I'm not as big as a barn door."

Ruth smiled, "Jess, I hope you didn't mind if I took things over. I think my place should be in the kitchen.

"Ruth, that's just how my parents worked. The family shared all the chores. We always worked together. Many hands make the load light; as the old saying goes."

Samuel woke Jiles David. He asked, "What time is it? I just went to sleep. What happened wagon?

"Jiles David, remember? We are staying with Jess. You haven't forgotten the husking bee have you?"

Jiles David yawned, rubbed his eyes and replied, "Oh yea dad, I remember now. Do I smell breakfast cooking? I'm starved."

"Get dressed Jiles, breakfast is ready."

Ruth had been working around the stove preparing the meal and asked, "Samuel, did you get as much sleep as I did? The bed was so very soft and inviting."

"You're telling me. That bed sure beats sleeping in that wagon, or worse, sleeping on the hard ground. I didn't realize just how tired I was. We had come quite a long way and we were completely worn out. This weary little family had about all it could take."

Ruth had put breakfast on the table and told the men to sit down and eat.

Jiles David came into the room, pulled up a chair, yawned, and sat down to his breakfast.

Ruth brought the coffee pot to the table and Jess prayed. "Heavenly Father, thank you for the food and also, less the hands that have prepared it. Thank you for sending this family to help me. I ask you to bless it in the name of Jesus."

Jess filled his plate and began to eat, commenting on how good everything tasted. He said, "I haven't food had this good since I don't know when. It sure is delicious. I get tired of my own cooking."

Ruth and Samuel laughed, saying, "Jess, I'm no better cook than you are. If it weren't for Ruth, I'd starve to death; I hate cooking.

When they had finished breakfast, Samuel asked, have you got all our chores lined up?"

Jiles David asked, "What do you have for me to do today Jess?"

"Tell you what you can do, why don't you get a pail of corn, go out to the chicken coop, and feed the chickens? I'll bet they are about starved. Then you can gather the eggs." Jiles David followed the men outside into the cool morning air.

The sun hadn't crested the horizon, and darkness still lingered, but signs of dawn, though faint, were there.

Jess went to the barn, lit a lantern, and he and Samuel began forking hay into the stalls.

Then Jess said, "Jiles David, why don't you milk the cow until its light enough to feed the chickens and gather their eggs. It won't be long before the sun comes up."

Jiles David followed Jess into the Jersey cow's stall and helped Jess get the milking stool and the wooden bucket. Jess asked, "Samuel, has he ever milked a cow before?"

"Oh yes, Jiles David is a pretty good hand around the farm. Our old place wasn't very big, but we did have a milk cow, and a few chickens, so he knows how."

"Okay then, Jiles David. Let's see what you can do." Jess stepped aside, handed him the bucket. Jiles David warmed his hands with his breath. The cow contentedly chewed her cud and lowed as Jiles David began milking her. Her lowing echoed throughout the barn and soon a cat showed up, meowing for the warm milk. Jiles David grinned at the cat and said, "Here puss, come and get a drink of milk." He playfully squirted it, and watched as the cat tried to get a drink.

Then Samuel said, "Ok, Jiles David, that's enough, save some milk for us!"

Jess and Samuel divided the hard chores between them, and labored throughout the day. Jiles David hauled some firewood to the house. He also helped feed and water the livestock. Ruth was in charge of the house and garden, while Jiles David helped where he could.

Chapter 6

It was late September, and the weather was changing. Subtle hints of the winter were beginning to appear. The leaves on the trees were changing, and in the mornings there was a hint frost on the ground. It was jacket weather, and some mornings when Jess went outside to tend to the chores the air was cold enough that he could see his own breath. He didn't like the coming of winter, with the ice and snow; it made doing the chores difficult.

The Wilson family proved to be a real God send, and he enjoyed their company. Their help with doing the chores made life much easier. It also was a comfort to him. They could never replace his family, but it did help to ease his loss. There were a few things that did get on his nerves though. One thing that bothered him was the way Ruth tried to rule the roost. He couldn't help but notice the way she constantly corrected Samuel if he made any kind of comment. It didn't matter what it was. It looked to him like Samuel was hen pecked. He couldn't help but like Samuel, but he wished he would put Ruth in her place for once. The constant fuss made over nothing was beginning to get on his nerves. He could feel a camp out coming in order to get some peace and quiet, but it would have to happen before cold weather set in.

Jess was glad for company, and knew that he shouldn't be complaining; but enough was enough. Perhaps he had lived alone for too long and just wasn't ready for the intrusion. The more Jess thought about it, the more convinced he was that a trip into the forest would be a good thing. Then Jess thought about the day that Bill Rolland had wandered by and stayed with him a few days. He had seemed to be a free spirit that didn't have any ties. He just went were he pleased when he pleased. The urge to get away for a while was growing, and it was becoming hard to stay put. He really struggled to make the right choice. He didn't want to abandon the farm, but he also didn't want to live with the Wilsons. He wanted his independence back, but hated the loneliness. He couldn't see a way to have the best of both worlds. He would have to choose one or the other. It was a real dilemma. Jess knew he could never abandon the farm, but it wouldn't hurt to get away for a short while.

As the days went by, Jess tried to push the idea of getting away for a day or two from his mind. He tried hard to ignore the way Ruth was taking over, working her will on them. It really got on his nerves. Every time he came into the house, she would say, "Now, don't forget to wipe your feet off." Ruth didn't say this in an angry tone of voice, but for some reason it grated on his nerves. Samuel didn't seem to mind, and acted like he hadn't heard her. "Perhaps I'm just being touchy because it's my home. He thought. "Whatever the reason was, Jess was getting more uncomfortable as the days went by. Jess was in a real dilemma. Before too long, winter would set in, and he would be trapped in the cabin for days on end. He didn't think he could stand that and the thought of leaving was looking better. If he did decide to leave, it would have to be soon.

It was about a week later on a Monday when Parson Walsh suddenly showed up. Jess had just come out of the barn and was not really all that surprised to see him. Parson Walsh said, "Well, good morning to you Jess." I happened to be in the neighborhood, and thought that I would drop by to see how you are getting along. I should have stopped by before this, but my circuit is a long one and it takes me a while to make it. Winter will set in before you know it, and that really restricts my travels."

Jess was glad to see Parson Walsh again, for he was very wise and he could confide in him. Jess told Parson Walsh to get off of his horse, and he would see if Ruth had a pot of coffee on. They went into the house, and as soon as Ruth saw them, the first thing out of her mouth was, "Why it's Parson Walsh. Wipe your feet off and come on in." Jess didn't say anything, but obeyed her command. Parson Walsh didn't seem to think anything about it, but just did as he was told.

Jess said, "Ruth, Parson Walsh could use a cup of coffee."

Samuel and Jiles David came in from outside. Jiles David had some stove wood, and just as soon as they stepped inside, Ruth said, "Don't forget to wipe your boots." Jess cringed at this, and thought to himself. "Why does Ruth do that? We know to wipe our feet by now?!" He looked over at Parson Walsh, and was really surprised to see him grinning. He said, "Ruth, you sure do have these men trained. I've never seen cleaner floors."

Ruth replied, "Parson, my mamma taught me that if you keep the floor clean the rest of the house would be easier to deal with, and she had it right."

Samuel laughed, "Parson, I'm just glad Ruth doesn't try and take over the barn and chicken coop. Boy would we be in trouble.

Parson Walsh laughed, and poked Jess in the ribs and said. "Jess, a woman makes a home what it is." Jess had to agree with him, but he still didn't like being reminded to wipe his feet. He tried to remember if his mother had done the same thing.

Ruth had gone to the stove to pour coffee for Parson Walsh, and then set sugar cookies on the table for him. As he partook of the repast, he began to ask how things were, and if he could help them.

"Parson, until Jess invited us to stay with him we were just about at our wits end. He was a God send. I don't know what we would have done if he hadn't taken us in.

Jess knew that Samuel and Ruth had their own way of doing things, and they seemed to get along. Personalities did clash sometimes, but it was just the way of things. He realized that it would be better if he tried to ignore Ruth's comments and do the best he could.

Jess asked Parson Walsh how long he was going to stay. He replied, "Well, Jess, not much longer. I have made a full circuit of the county and it's just about time to make my way home. I've been gone quite long enough. I miss my family. His comment about family struck a chord with Jess, and he began to feel sorry that he wasn't more tolerant of Ruth.

Samuel said, "okay, come on Jiles David, we have more wood to chop." Jess excused himself and went out with them to help with the fire wood.

Ruth was puttering around in the kitchen cleaning the breakfast dishes.

Parson Walsh set his cup down and asked, "Ruth, your family seems to have settled in just fine. How are things going?"

"Well Parson, Jess has been a good host. We are very thankful that he took us in. I don't know what we would have done without him. But to be honest with you, he seems to be restless. He is very good to us, and has allowed us to come and go as we please. But there are times when I think we are getting on his nerves. Jess has mentioned he might go hunting. We have plenty of food put away, and gathering the fire wood is all but done. I think that he just wants to be alone before the weather turns to bad. I don't blame him. Perhaps our situation will change.

Parson Walsh knew when he asked Jess to take the

Wilson family in, personalities might clash, but that was just the way of life and was bound to happen. But as far as he could tell, Jess seemed to be taking it all in stride.

He said, "Ruth, as you know, Jess has had a tough ordeal in losing his family and I don't think he will ever really get over it. Whether he realizes it or not, you folks have been a God send. If Jess goes off on his own for a while, just remember to pray for him. I think the longing for his family and for something of his own weighs heavy on his mind. I am going home today before the weather turns bad, and I thought that I had better see how things were going. Just be patient and trust God. Your situation will change, and Jesse's situation will also; although it may take some time."

Jess and Samuel were out chopping the remaining fire wood while Jiles David stacked it next to the house.   Parson Walsh sat on a stump in the yard and listened to the ring of the ax as it struck the wood. As he sat, a cold breeze sprang up. He looked skyward at the clouds, and a few snowflakes started to fall. This was not unexpected at all. He knew the snowfall wouldn't last long, but it did signal the approach of winter. It was time to go to home to his own family.

Parson Walsh watched as the dusting of snow began to accumulate on the ground and on the tops of the fence posts. If the clouds had contained any more moisture, they could get a real snowfall, but he could tell that this would be short lived, but it still prompted him to start for home. He got up off of the stump and walked to where the men were chopping firewood, gathered a few sticks and helped David stack it.

When Jiles David saw Parson Walsh helping him, he remarked, "Say, Parson, thanks a lot for helping me. Did you see it snowing? I sure hope it keeps it up. I want to make a snowman."

Parson Walsh laughed, and said, "Jiles David, I don't really think it will snow much, but, you never know, it could."

After the firewood was cut, Parson Walsh said that he had better be going, and that he had a long way to go before nightfall.

Jess grasped his extended hand thanking him for all that he had done. They went back inside, and Parson Walsh prayed with them.

Ruth had packed a lunch to help him on his way; they went out onto the porch and watched him saddle His horse they bid him God speed and watched as the snowflakes swirled all around the horse as he headed up the lane and out of site.

Ruth went back in the house while Jess and Samuel lingered a while longer, watching the snow fall.

"Jess, he said, I don't think this snow will stay on the ground for long. It's still a bit too warm. The temperature is fluctuating too much."

Jess agreed and said, "You know Samuel, this just might be a good time for me to go on the hunting trip I have been talking about. We have the main chores caught up, and I'm way past due for a break from all of the work around here. Could you spare me for a little while?"

Chapter 7

Jess was more than ready for his hunting trip. The days remained cold in the mornings, but by mid-morning it warmed up a little.

The weather in late fall could be fickle at times, and a snow storm might blow in at any moment, but it never lasted for more than a day. Jess wasn't concerned with the weather, and it wasn't long before he had everything ready for his jaunt into the woods.

The day that Jess left, proved to be cold, but that didn't bother him at all. His desire to get away for a while was great, and a little bit of cold air wasn't going to be a hindrance. He saddled the roan, placed his bedroll behind the saddle along with his camping gear, put his foot in the stirrup and settled into the ride. "Come on Sal, let's get out of here." Sal stomped her feet and shook her head as if she understood his words. Jess pointed her in the right direction, headed across the fields and towards the woods. The saddle squeaked as he rocked with the rhythmic sway of the horse. A smile began creasing his face as he rode across the field.

The pleasantness of the morning, the interaction with Sal, began to take over; he soon put all thoughts of the farm behind him.

"This is freedom!" Jess said, as he reached down and patted Sal. "That's a girl, Sal you look like you are enjoying this as much as me." Jess rode along until reaching the treeline, then stopped just long enough to determine which trail he wanted to use. There were two or three trails to choose from and after a few moments he chose the middle one and plunged into the woods and followed along this trail for a few hundred yards or so until he came to a small stream. He watered Sal, and let her feed upon the foliage growing nearby.

Jess followed the streams winding course until he came across a parcel of ground with a small clearing in it.

"It's a perfect campsite Sal." Jess got off Sal, led her into the clearing, and let her graze while he began clearing a spot for his camp.

Jess gathered some stones together for his camp fire, then unsaddled Sal, rubbed her down, and set up the tent and began to settle into camp life.

It was still early in the morning and Jess had a pot of coffee on the fire and the aroma of wood smoke and coffee soon filled the air. He had only brought a few things to sustain him while he camped, such as flour, lard, and some bacon, but he intended, for the most part, to hunt. He might set some snares to catch rabbits, or perhaps shoot a squirrel now and then, and if he happened upon a small deer, he would add that to his larder. All in all, his plan was to relax, and not get caught up in to much hunting or doing very much work. He just wanted to get away.

While the coffee was making, Jess tossed some of the bacon in the skillet, and began to smile because of the freedom he was feeling. 'It doesn't get better than this," he thought.

Sal, who wasn't tethered came up behind him and began to nuzzle his neck. He spoke to her in soothing tones, and scratched her ears. Then Jess went to the saddle bags and scooped out some corn. She nickered at Jess and began eating. It seemed that Sal was enjoying the camp out also.

After Jess had eaten, he cleaned up the skillet, stored it away in the tent and just sat back. It wasn't long before he drifted off to sleep. He had pulled a log from the edge of the clearing and used it as a seat. He was stretched out on the ground in front of it, and the sound of contented snoring soon drifted into the air.

As often happens in the northern climes of Ohio,

the weather suddenly began to change. First it began to sprinkle rain. Jess awakened out of his slumber and sat up and looked around. He saw that dark clouds were gathering, and as the raindrops fell, a slight breeze began to blow. It wasn't at all that unexpected. Jess rather relished the change in the weather. As long as it didn't snow, all would be well. He got up off of the ground, and gathered some more firewood. This he placed under the low hanging boughs of a pine tree so that if bad weather did set in, his supply of fuel wouldn't get very wet.

As Jess worked, he stirred the coals of the fire for warmth. Sal had drifted away from camp and was cropping grass at the fringe of the woods. When Jess gathered the firewood, he called to her and said "Come on in Sal, I think it's high time that we went exploring."

The rain continued sprinkling down, but it wasn't long until the clouds parted; allowing a few rays of sunshine shine in. Jess stopped what he was doing, and observed the scene.

"Now this, he said out loud, is what I'm talking about. Sal, let's get saddled up and go for that ride."

Sal nickered, and pawed at the ground as Jess put the blanket and saddle on. He placed his rifle in the scabbard, mounted up, then guided Sal to the woods and entered a dim trail. The trees were dripping with moisture, and he had to dodge around low-lying limbs to keep from getting a shower, but he didn't mind at all, it was just a part of horseback riding.

As Jess advanced, he closely observed the ground, looking for a deer trail. At one point a turtle was making its way along the path. Sal unconcernedly side stepped the turtle and continue following its twisting course through the trees.

At one point it dipped down into a ravine and up a steep slope on the other side.

Jess sat up in the saddle, grabbed the saddle horn and said, "Git up Sal." she lunged up the slope and into the trees at the top. As he sat there, he began looking around. It was then that Jess noticed an abandoned camp and there was a fire pit and an old house.

He got off the horse and began looking around to see what he could find. As he examined the area, he realized that it was an Indian village. The Indians were gone, and Jess wondered if this had been Gray Wolf's home.

As Jess walked around the old village, he found some items that had been left behind. There was a pair of worn out moccasins. He picked them up, examined them and began to wonder who had worn them. What a sad event it must have been for the Indian who had made them. Instead of working with the Indians, the government had forced them off of their land because of greed.

Jess continued searching for items the Indians had left behind, and found some arrowheads. These he kept as momentous of their sad passing. "I wonder how I would have reacted, if someone had said to me, you don't live here, get out?" Jess shook his head and then thought of Grey Wolf. "No wonder he was so angry. Our people had destroyed his way of life and taken away everything he had known."

Jess began to think that something should be done for him. But what could one man do?

As he looked around the area, a thought dropped into his mind. It was a bold thought, but not an impossible one. The longer Jess pondered on it the more he realized that the loneliness was coming to a head, and that it should be put to good use; so, he began to formulate a plan. The camping trip had been just what he needed to finally clear his mind. Jess continued to look around trying to get a better feel for the Indians, hoping to get an insight into their lives.

The more he lingered, the more he got a sense of the deprivations they went through just to live.

It was true, that his family had struggled through difficult times to eke out a living, but nothing like what the Indians must have been up against and what they were going through now. Their displacement was so unnecessary, and could have been avoided.

Jess took one last look around, saddled up, and continued on his journey along the narrow path, the whole time considering the thought that had dropped in his mind. A smile creased his face as he pondered. He could see a way to help at least one Indian. It was just the beginning of a plan.

The more Jess thought about his idea, the greater his determination became to set it in motion. It would have to be worked out, but Jess knew it could be carried through as long as he stayed focused.

As Jess rode, he took his time, letting Sal stop whenever she wanted to. There was no hurry, and so he continued on in this manner until afternoon.

Jess happened upon a spot that was close to a stream, he removed Sal's saddle, led her to the water and let her drink. Jess cleared a likely area of leaves, gathered a few stones together, and got some kindling

Soon wood smoke was rising through the trees. Jess added larger pieces of wood to the fire, and made ready to cook some lunch.

As Jess sat by the fire, he wondered what Parson Walsh would think of his plan; or, for that matter, what his dad would think about it. His mom and dad had a true pioneer spirit, and had carved a home out of the wilderness. Was what he wanted to do any different?

Jess stayed at this camp until rather late in the afternoon. He had tethered Sal close to the creek so she wouldn't wander off. He began hunting, hoping that he would find some game close by. There wasn't a great need of food as yet, but if he happened upon a deer, it would come in handy later on. The weather was just cool enough so that the meat wouldn't spoil. After taking one last look around the camp, he entered the woods.

As soon as his feet hit the path, he began to wonder how many Indians had trod the same path over the years.

Jess moved along the trail until he came upon a dense glen. The leaves had all fallen from the large oak trees, and it seemed to be a place of reverence. It was very quiet; not even a bird was singing. Then he spotted an earthen mound that had small trees growing around it. As he approached the mound, he saw that someone had built an arching rock entrance in the mound. The rocks had been carefully lain so as to form a covering. It was obvious that this was a burial mound.   No doubt it was for a very important person. Jess removed his hat in order to show respect to the Indian who had been buried there. He began wondering if the Indians spirit was still lingering near, for the hushed silence of that place seemed to be closing in. Jess decided that he wouldn't hunt in that scared place.   He turned around and went back; humbled by what he had just found. The experience helped make up his mind as to what should be done.

When Jess walked back into the clearing, he looked up at the sky. It was getting a little late in the day, and there were dark clouds gathering. It looked like snow. He didn't want to get caught out in a snow storm, so, Jess saddled Sal, and headed back to camp and to his tent.

The camp didn't look like it was disturbed as he emerged from the trees, so he rode in. He took the saddle and blanket off of Sal and rubbed her down. She stood still and nibbled on some of the grass growing there.

When Jess finished, he put the saddle and blanket in the tent, and began making ready for nightfall. As he worked around the camp, a cool breeze sprang up, bringing a few drops of moisture. What he feared would happen, did. It started snowing. The snow was not unexpected, but there was absolutely no telling how long an early snow like this would last. Jess cut some poles, tied them together with several thick spruce boughs and fashioned them on top of the poles to help keep the snow off of the tent as much as possible.

The snow seemed to increase in volume, and it didn't look like it would let up any time soon. After he had finished securing the tent, Jess got Sal and tethered her under a nearby evergreen that had dense limbs. He then gathered as much winter grass for her as possible, and then began looking to his fire, stirring up any coals that remained from that morning. It wasn't very long before he had a blazing fire. It sizzled and popped each time snowflakes fell into the flames.

Jess worked around the camp preparing against the cold to come. As he did this the wind suddenly began blowing harder, and the volume of snow increased. Jess had to put on another coat. He knew that it wouldn't be long before he would have to retreat into the tent, so he checked on Sal to see how she was faring. Sal didn't seem to mind the snow. Her shelter under the tree was adequate and the horse looked quite content. Jess added more fuel fire to keep the fire hot, he couldn't to let it burn out if the temperature happened to plunge.

As darkness fell, Jess prepared his supper and sat in the entrance of the tent contentedly eating.

The snowstorm proved to be short- lived, but had deposited an inch of snow anyway, but not enough to be a bother. Fortunately the temperature hadn't dipped down at all, but remained constant.

Jess finished eating his supper, then added more wood to the fire, and as darkness closed in he checked on Sal once more, and made ready for the night.

The next day Jess awakened with a start. It was very quiet; too quiet. He lay still just listening. It was still dark outside, and he was reluctant to get out of his bed roll, but nature called, and so he got out of bed, got dressed, pulled his boots on and then went outside. The temperature had dropped. He retrieved his coat and hat and stirred up the coals, and tossed on some kindling. The flames flared up, and Jess quickly put on a pot of coffee to warm his bones.

As he waited for the coffee, he sat by the fire and waited for sunrise. When the coffee began to boil, it sounded loud in the stillness of the surrounding forest.

Soon, he heard Sal whinny, so he got up from the fire, and with cup in hand, walked over to where she stood under the tree. Sal nuzzled him and he almost spilt his coffee. Jess unfastened her from the tether and she went straight to the stream, and began to get her fill of water. Jess went back to the fire and soaked in its warmth.

The sun rise brought a cold breeze, and a little more snow, but it soon passed, for the snow clouds dissipated before the warmth of the sun. Jess took stock of his surroundings, and saw that the snow wasn't very deep at all; so the first thing he did was set a snare. Then Jess went back to camp and cooked breakfast.

By the time Jess had finished eating, the sun had crested, and the temperature had begun to rise. He hoped that the day would prove to be successful, because he intended ride. The last thing that Jess needed was to get more snow, but he knew that the slight snowfall was really only a hint of the weather to come. He wanted to take advantage of the weather as it was.

Jess made sure that Sal was well fed from the feed he had brought, and while she munched on the grain, he rubbed her down, and checked her hooves for any problems, and then put the blanket and saddle on her.

"Okay old girl, don't you think it's about time we went for a ride?" Sal let Jess put the bit in her mouth and she impatiently stomped her feet as if in reply. Jess scratched her ears and smiled at the thought of hitting the trail through the woods again.

The day was perfect, and it was warming up. The clouds had passed, and the sun was shining bright. He could feel the joy of living coursing through his veins as he saddled up and rode down the trail. Jess headed for the abandoned Indian camp he had explored the day before, but this time, instead of stopping, he followed the dim twisting trail down an incline, and to the glens beyond.

As he reached the trees of this secluded place, a hush fell. The glen reminded him of a cathedral. The trees were covered in snow, and were very majestic, beautiful, holy looking. It was no wonder the Indians fought to keep their land.

As Jess observed the hallowed surroundings, he became determined to follow through with his plan. It might not come about until spring thaw, but it would happen. He was sure of it. Jess rode on into the middle of the majestic trees, and just enjoyed the quiet solitude.

After a long while, Jess left the spire of the snow-covered trees and continued on down the trail. He meandered along the trails, just exploring, enjoying the ride.

It was late into the morning, when Jess suddenly remembered the snares he had set. He reluctantly turned Sal around and started back to camp. He couldn't complain, for he had ridden quite a ways.

By the time he got to camp, he would be ready

to eat some lunch, and As Jess got closer to camp, he got off of Sal and approached one of his snares.   Sure enough there was a rabbit in one of them. He retrieved the animal and walked Sal.

"Wood smoke, I smell wood smoke. I just knew I put the fire out." He made his way to the edge of the trees, and cautiously peered around a tree trunk. Someone was sitting on the log by the fire. He studied the person for a few minutes, and then stepped out of the trees.   Upon hearing Jess, the stranger stood up. Jess was surprised to see Caleb Springer at his fire.

"Well, I'll be dogged, it's Caleb Springer. What brings you into this neck of the woods?"

"I was wondering whose camp this was," he said. "I might ask you the same question Jess. What are you up to?"

Jess laughed, "Oh, I just wanted to get away before the weather changes for good."

"Me too,"   "I figured that whoever's camp this was had to come back sooner or later, so I built the fire, and made myself to home."

Jess got the coffee pot, and made some fresh coffee.   He said, "Nothing but the best coffee for a guest."

Caleb remarked, "Yes, I could use a hot cup of coffee.   I've been out for a good while. I wanted to track down a deer for the larder back home.   You never know how severe a winter we are going to have."

"Boy, you can say that again! It has been snowing off and on. It wasn't much, but you never know. There might come a big blizzard at any time."

Caleb looked around and commented on the stack of firewood under the tree. "Tell me Jess, are you planning on staying? You have a lot of firewood."

"Well, I just about worked myself down at home. I finally decided that I needed a break. Sometimes, the walls start closing in. I just packed up and came out here to camp for a few days."

"That happens to me too, Caleb replied. "I just have to get away from the work, and hunting is as good an excuse as any."

"Yes it is, and if you follow the creek for a ways, you are bound to come across a deer."

"Well, I just might do that. I haven't quite made up my mind if I want to kill one."

They continue in this vein of conversation until a sudden movement caught Caleb's eye. He said, "Jess, don't move. There is a big old skunk coming. He must have smelled the camp."

Jess replied, "If that thing sprays us, we are in big trouble. It's next to impossible to get the smell off."

They held their breath as the skunk came closer and closer to them. When it reached their position by the fire, it hesitated for a moment and advanced a little bit closer, and lifted its tail. Nothing happened. The skunk got close to the camp fire, sniffed around a few times, went past Jess and Caleb and into the tent.

"I can't believe this Caleb. That skunk had better not spray in there. I'll have to toss everything away."

"Well Jess, there ain't much you can do about it now."

They couldn't help but laugh about the touchy situation, so they stayed put until the skunk decided to leave. It seemed like hours before the skunk had satisfied its curiosity and came waddling out of the tent and then went in the woods. Jess gave a big sigh of relief and went the tent and looked around. He couldn't find anything wrong, except for the faint smell of skunk. He counted himself lucky that he had gotten off so easy.

Caleb lingered around the camp a while longer and then stated, "I had better get. This weather might change."

Jess started to ask how Abigail was, but didn't. Instead, he asked, "How are the folks doing? I really need to get over there and say hello."

Caleb was well aware of his sister Abigail's attraction to Jess, but he didn't mention this, so he replied, "Well, Jess, everyone is just fine, although Abigail had a horse step on her foot a while back, and Mathew fell out of a tree. But other than that they are just fine. You really should drop by. You haven't been around since the shucking bee."

"Caleb, you know that the Wilson's have been living with me don't you? I have been pretty busy with them, but I'll ride over your way before the weather turns bad. I'm not going to stay here much longer; I need to get back home. Tell your folks hello for me, and that I'll drop by before long.

The two talked for a moment longer, then Caleb, who had tethered his horse down by the creek, mounted up, waved at Jess, and then rode away into the woods.

Jess was thinking about the Springers. He knew that they were there for him, but he still had a great longing for his own family, and the comfort they brought. It was obvious to him that he couldn't continue living the way he currently was. He wanted more, and began thinking about Abigail, and what a fine person she was. He really did like her, but was kind of afraid of a relationship. What if he got involved and she was suddenly taken away like his family had been? Jess didn't know if he could endure another tragedy. Besides, he had made up his mind to try and find Grey Wolf if possible, and offer him a parcel of land to live on. It the Wilsons watched over the farm for a while, everything would work out; he could go ahead with his plan.

When he returned, then maybe then he could think about a relationship.

Jess felt better about his situation, getting away from the farm had been just the thing he needed. It had been like a breath of fresh air. He now had a plan; a purpose. He had no idea about the outcome, but after seeing the Indian camp, and the burial mound, it made him want to do something to try and rectify the Indians loss. He may never get to find Grey Wolf, but he felt he must try. He also knew that he must visit Abigail before he left, and perhaps confide in her.   He did like her, but felt that the time hadn't come to get very serious. He hated to take a wait and see attitude, but it would be better than making promises he might not be able to keep.

Jess looked around the camp, and decided to stay on one more night and then head for home. He retrieved the rabbit he had snared, and began to dress it for his lunch.   He got a stick, and skewered it. He placed the rabbit between two forked sticks and began to roast it. It would be a meager meal, but enough to get by on until supper.

By late afternoon, the temperature began to drop again, so Jess put more wood on the fire and waited to see what nature had in store.   Sal had started stomping her feet, and shaking her head. Evidently she sensed a change.   The temperature had dropped, but Jess couldn't tell if there was more snow on the way. There were dark clouds in the sky but everything seemed quiet and calm. Even the birds were quiet. This alone should have been a warning to him.

Jess had been puttered around, confident that all was well. He wanted to camp out just one more night and then head home in the morning. He was well rested, and ready to go back to the farm.

Jess cooked supper and sat back against the log. He had just poured another cup of coffee when a cold breeze suddenly sprang up. It had a bite to it so Jess tossed another log on the fire.

Sal snorted and began prancing around. Jess got up and walked over to her. "What's the matter Sal, are you nervous?" The horse seemed ill at ease, and Jess began to Stroke her neck trying to reassure her.

As Jess calmed Sal, sleet began falling. It only lasted for a moment. Then, the wind started to blow, rattling tree limbs.

The wind was sharp. Jess began to realize that they were in for a harsh night. He got Sal's saddle blanket and put it on her to insure she stayed warm. Jess tossed some more wood on the fire, and went in the tent.

The sound of the falling sleet was loud as it struck the ground and the trees. The camp fire sizzled and sputtered, and white smoke arose as the sleet hit the flames.

Jess felt quite helpless in the tent, he just hoped it didn't collapse. He would be in a real fix. The only thing to be done was to wait out the storm, and keep the fire going. The sleet continued battering Jess's tent, and then the temperature dropped, and the sleet turned into ice.

Jess stuck his head out of the tent trying to see if Sal was okay, but it was so dark that he couldn't see a thing, and he got hit with ice pellets. He withdrew his head, sat back, and prayed that the tent held up. There was nothing else he could do. Jess felt helpless.

Sal was tethered under the tree, and was safe enough, but still got hit by ice. She kept close to the tree trunk, and waited out the storm.

Jess could hear the tree limbs cracking, and presently an overburdened limb snapped off of a tree nearby, causing a shower of ice to hit his tent. The boughs began to sag under the weight.

Jess couldn't do thing about it. He hoped and prayed that his shelter didn't collapse on top of him. The storm wasn't showing signs of letting up; if anything,

It was worse; the wind howled around the trees, scattering loose ice crystals everywhere.

Suddenly, a very large tree toppled over and came crashing down close to where Sal was tethered. She lunged away, breaking the tether. Jess grabbed a lantern, put boots on, got his coat and hat then ran into the storm. Sal was nowhere to be seen. He tried calling, but to no avail. The din of the raging storm drowned out his voice. He stood under the shelter of the tree for a while, but finally had to give up and go back to the tent.

Sal, had run from the danger of the falling tree, and had pushed her way into some thick over hanging limbs in the woods that were a hundred yards or so from the camp. Here she stayed, trying to avoid the ice. She still had her blanket on for Jess had secured it. It was a familiar comfort, and helped to ward off the ice.

It was getting rather late, and the ice storm continued its battering force. Jess was beginning to think it would never end, but the wind suddenly died down. The ice lessoned somewhat, and then stopped all together and an eerie silence fell over the landscape. Jess had no idea of the time. All he knew was, that the storm had stopped and that the sky was cloud covered, for there were no stars to be seen. He got the lamp again, and tried to start a fire. This was not an easy thing to do, but fortunately for him, he had put kindling in the tent just in case. He cleared the ice away from his fire pit, gathered what dry firewood that was left and built the fire. The first thing he did was to put on another pot of coffee, for he was shivering from the cold.

While the coffee was making, he began calling for Sal trying to coax her to the fire. He went to the tree she had been under, but the only thing he found was the rope. He continued calling, hoping she would come in.

He gave up and went back to the fire and waited to see if Sal would come in. The cold was intense, but the wind had died down. Jess stomped his feet and swung his arms help to keep his circulation going. He kept this up until the sunrise. The ice on the trees and ground glistened in the suns light. The ice had taken down several of the trees and many limbs. If he had pitched his tent in the woods instead of the clearing, he might not have survived. He began to wonder if Sal had made it through the night or not. He called to her a few times, but all that met him was silence.

After the sun had crested the trees, Jess began hunting for Sal. He could see where she had bolted through the trees, for the ice was much disturbed. Jess began calling to her again, and it wasn't long before he heard her nicker. He followed the sound, and finally found her backed up under low-lying limbs in some dense undergrowth. She didn't look any worse for the ware, but Jess examined her just to make sure. He calmed her and then led her back to the fire.

Before Jess could leave the camp, he had to make sure that the trail he had come in on was passable. He left Sal and ventured into the woods. There was quite a bit of damage, but the trail wasn't that bad. Tree limbs were arched from the weight of ice. They sparkled brightly giving the woods a majestic glow. It was very beautiful to see.

Jess had to get away from the danger of the ice because. A tree might come crashing down; trapping him underneath. If that happened, he might never be found. He went back to camp and began packing for the dangerous trip home. He saddled Sal, put his tent behind the saddle and started down the icy trail.

The trip out of the woods proved to be a challenge, and he had to lead Sal through some of the worst places.

When they got to the creek, it was clear, and easy to cross. But on the other side of the creek, the trail became more difficult to navigate. Jess had to dismount Sal several times to avoid getting hit by overburdened tree limbs. They were continually showered by ice shards and Jess had to brush them away.

It was around noon when Jess emerged from the icy tangle. The ice was everywhere, but, it was slowly melting. September was a month when the weather could surprise you. The storm had been one of those surprises. If the temperature kept on rising, the ice would be gone in a day or two. Jess started across the fields and homeward, and it wasn't long before he could see smoke curling out of the chimney. He began to think of the warm fire and the steaming hot coffee. He was eager to get back and start making plans for his trip.

When Jess rode into the yard, Jiles David, who had been gathering eggs, saw Jess, and proclaimed, "Jess, Dad said he might look for you today if you didn't show up.

Jess smiled as he dismounted and replied, "You know Jiles David, there was a time or two I thought the ice would get me. But do you know what? God must have been looking out for me, because, except for some close calls, we weathered the storm. Jiles David, I have to give Sal a rub down, and get some feed into her. She is all worn out. I'll come inside in just a little while."

Jess led Sal to the barn, forked her some hay and then gave her the much needed rub down.

When Jess finished taking care of Sal, he started looking around for any damage that might have occurred while he was gone, but everything seemed intact. He went up onto the porch, started to go in, but he hesitated, knowing Ruth would be at the door.

Surprisingly enough, he didn't mind.   He removed his boots, and left them by the door, and went inside.

Ruth, who had come into the kitchen proclaimed, "Well, Jess, were glad to see you made it through the ice storm okay. Samuel thought he was going to have to go out and start hunting for you today."

"To tell you the truth, I wondered if I was going to get out alive. That ice storm came out of nowhere. Sal bolted in the night, and I had to go looking for her this morning, but we made it out. Is that coffee I smell? I'm starved and still a little cold!"

Ruth poured him a cup of coffee and then said, "Jess I've got some homemade bread and jam you can have, that should hold you over until dinner." Jess gladly took the snack and went to the hearth and warmed himself. The longer that Jess sat by the warm fire, the more tired he became. The sleepless night was catching up with him and before long he began to nod off. Ruth got a blanket and covered him up. She watched for Jiles David and Samuel, to warn them to keep quiet. Sure enough she heard Jiles David coming up on the porch. She met him at the door and whispered for him to be still so as not to wake Jess. He complied with her wishes and tiptoed into the kitchen. A little while later Samuel came in and was met with the same instructions.

It was past supper time when Jess finally woke. He rubbed his eyes and looked around.
At first he didn't know where he was until he saw the hearth, and smelled food.   Ruth had him set a plate of food aside, and he ate heartily.

Samuel and Jiles David had been bringing in wood, and Samuel proclaimed, "Jess, I'm glad you made it back. Did you get rested?"

"Yes I did. I guess I was worn out. I didn't even make it to my bed. How did you folks fare?
"Oh, we made it just fine, as long as we stayed in."

"When I rode in I couldn't see anything damaged by the ice storm."

"Everything held together. The animals made it just fine. The livestock made it into the barn, and stayed there. Other than a few tree limbs, there was no real damage done."

"I'm so glad to hear that. You should have been with me out in the woods. There were several trees down, not to mention all of the limbs that broke off." Sal broke took off, but she didn't go very far. I found her backed up under some trees trying to get away from the ice. We were fortunate to get out of there in one piece, but God saw us through it all.

Jess almost divulged his plan about Grey Wolf, but changed his mind. The timing didn't feel right. He had made up his mind, and was going through with it, but not until spring. He had plenty of time between now and then to discuss leaving. But he thought about telling Charles Springer about his plan. There was Abigail to think of. He was sure that she liked him, but there was no way to see how things would turn out.

September, with all of its varied weather, didn't surprise Jess at all. On the last week of the month, the temperature seemed balmy, but Jess knew that they were just spring like days, and that the drudgery of the long cold winter days would start. Jess looked at the warm weather as a sign that it was past time visit the Springers. He had said he would visit them, and took advantage of the warm days.

"Jiles David, did you wipe your feet when you came in?" Yes mamma I did," he replied.

"Well, you know how I am. This is Jesse's home.

"Samuel laughed and said, "Jess, I wish you could have seen Ruth when we loaded everything into that old wagon of ours. I thought she was going to have the nervous riggers trying to keep it clean."

Jess couldn't help but laugh, and said, "I can only

imagine how it was. What was it like camping on the trail?" Jess surprised himself. He had always hated it when Ruth got fussy. But now, he understood. She was only trying to make up for his hospitality. Now he felt bad for complaining about Ruth's ways.

After having breakfast, Jess spoke up and said, "I have to go over to the Springers this morning, and I'm not sure how long I'll be gone. Don't expect me for Lunch. It is about five miles over there. The weather is so nice, that I thought I had better take advantage of it."

Jiles David asked, "Jess, do you need me to keep you company? I'd be glad to go with you."

Jess smiled and thanked him for the offer. "Well now Jiles David, who is going to look after things while I'm gone? Tell you what I'll do. When I come back, and if it isn't too late, I'll let you ride Sal if you want to. How does that sound?"

Jiles David enthusiastically replied, "Really Jess? Boy I can't wait!"

Jess looked at Samuel, and winked. "Why, Jiles David, I'll bet you get a horse of your own sometime. Until then, and if your dad and mom don't care, you can look after Sal, and ride her once in a while. Is it a deal?"

Jiles David, grinning from ear to ear said, "It's a deal."

Jess made his way to the barn, saddled Sal and rode up the lane, and little puffs of dust trailed behind the horse's hooves. Jess breathed deeply of the fresh fall air; taking in the colorful cornucopia of falling leaves. It was a good day to ride, and he reveled in the freedom it brought. He urged Sal into a loping gate, and they fairly flew up the lane and out onto the main road. Jess halted Sal and looked down the road just in time to see a herd of deer with tails in the air. Jess laughed as they bounded away and disappeared out of sight. Jess started up the road, but there wasn't a real reason to get in a hurry, so he relaxed into the ride.

When Jess finally arrived at the Springers house, he saw Marta coming from the well house with a bucket of water for the kitchen. She stopped, got a better grip on the bucket, and welcomed Jess. She smiled and said, "I'll be, it's Jess. Hitch your horse to the rail and come on in. I'll put some coffee on. Did you eat yet?"

Jess laughed at her greeting, and replied, "I had my breakfast early this morning, but I would take some coffee, and if you happen to have a little jam and bread I'd take some of that too. It must be getting close to my lunch time anyway."

Marta replied, "The men are probably around here somewhere, probably in the field. Why don't you go and try to find them while I start their lunch?"

Jess got off of Sal, led her to the watering trough and let her drink her fill. Then he tied her to the hitching rail, and headed for the barn. There wasn't anyone in there, and he noticed that the team and wagon was gone. He followed the road past the barn and into the field beyond. In the distance he could see the wagon. It looked like Charles, Matthew, and Caleb was examining the field.

When Jess walked up to them, Charles greeted him and said, "Jess, what brings you to our neck of the woods? Are you hungry?"

Jess laughed and said, "How did you guess that I was thinking about Marta's cooking?

No, I'm kidding, I thought I would ride over this way to check on you and to see if you had any damage from the ice storm we had a while back."

Charles replied, "We did get a little a little bit of damage, but not as bad as I thought it was going to be. It's a good thing the apple seeds didn't sprout.

Caleb and Matthew were trimming some broken limbs off of an oak, and tossing them onto a fire. Caleb stopped long enough to join in the conversation to say, "Jess the other day, when you were camping, I hunted, for a while, but then I went on home. I had gotten out of the woods and across the field just as the ice storm hit.   I got pelted pretty hard a few times. I just made it back into the barn when the sleet changed into ice.   I wondered how you were doing out there. I'm glad you made it back in one piece. That was a very bad storm."

Jess said, "Well, we did okay, until some tree limbs began falling everywhere. Sal got loose, but I found her huddled under some trees. I had some difficulty getting out of the woods, but managed to get out unharmed."

After all the trimming of dead limbs was done, Charles told Matthew to put the tools in the wagon. He gathered them up and they got in, and headed back to the house. On the way, Jess spoke up and said, "Charles, there is something I want to talk to you about. It's the real reason I came over today."

"Sure Jess, what can I help you with?"

"Well, to be honest with you, I have a story to tell, and I need your advice.   I am taking a trip, and don't know when I'll be back."

"Okay Jess, I will help you all I can. Why don't we wait until we get back to the house? We can discuss it then."

"That would be great Charles, I appreciate it.

Matthew heard Jess say he was going to go on a trip, and as soon as they got back, the first thing he did, was to tell Abigail and Ruth that Jess was leaving.

When Jess and Charles got to the house, Jess went over to Abigail, he asked, "How are you doing? I came over see if everyone made it through the ice storm."

At first Abigail didn't answer, but then she looked him in the eyes and asked him, "Jess, why are you leaving us? I wish you wouldn't go." She immediately blushed and then grew silent.

Jess knew that Abigail wasn't prying; she was just concerned. It touched his heart, and so he replied, "Well Abigail, there is a journey I feel I must take, and you might as well hear what I have to say. He started with the death of his parents, and then told her about how lonely he had been. Then he told about Grey Wolf, and how that he felt responsible for his welfare, and that it was his Christian duty to find him, and restore a part of his peoples land; even if it was only a few acres.

Abigail stated, "Jess, that the most noble thing that I ever heard. There are few people that would have compassion, especially for Indians. We seem to forget that they were here before us. I hope you succeed in finding him."

Marta spoke up and said, "Jess, are you really sure you want to do this? What if bad things happen? "Now Marta, Jess can handle himself. I'm more worried about Sal than anything. Jess, do you think Sal is up to the trip?"

"Just like a man," retorted Marta, "Charles is more concerned about that horse than he is about Jess!"

Jess couldn't help but laugh, and said he would be okay. He thanked them for listening to his story, and said that he hadn't told the Wilsons yet, but that he would tell them his plans and make arrangements.

Then he asked, "Charles, I'm planning on going this spring or summer, and if for some reason the Wilsons move out, do you think it would be possible for someone to look after things?

Charles responded by saying, "Jess, there is a lot of work to be done, but we can work something out. When you tell the Wilsons, have Samuel let me know if they plan on leaving; that way we can look in on your place. We might even bring your milk cow over here. The hogs and other animals should be alright, but we will check on them for you. As for the haying, and other chores, we will just have to work that out as best we can."

Jess thanked them, and said he couldn't imagine getting along without neighbors.

It was well into the afternoon when Jess finally decided it was past time to go home.

It had been quite an enjoyable day, and he had helped them with the chores. Abigail had made certain to visit with Jess as much as possible. The kiss they had shared lingered in her mind, and she would like to know Jess better. She followed him outside and said, "Jess, I sacked up a loaf of homemade bread for you, I hope you enjoy it."

"Why thank you Abigail, I'm sure will. You must be reading my mind. I wanted some more of your mother's bread; but didn't want to ask. I'll have to stop by again sometime, and see how she makes it. Whenever I try to make bread it turns out hard as a rock."

Abigail looked him, smiled, and said, "Jess you can come over here anytime you want. I'll show you how to make bread; it is easy.

Jess felt a warm sensation wash over him. He thought, "Why, Abigail is flirting with me."

He smiled at her and replied, "Abigail, I would like that very much. I'm not a very good cook."
It's a good thing that the Wilsons are living with me. I might starve to death."

"Oh, Jess, I don't think you have to worry about starving, just as long as you have us for neighbors." She held the bag of bread out to him. He reached for it, and she pretended to drop the bag so that he had to grasp her hand. Abigail squeezed Jesse's hand and

looked at him, then smiled.   Jess got her message.
He wanted to kiss her, but not on the porch; so, he did the next best thing.   He held onto her soft hand and said, "Oh, stand still for a minute Abigail. You have something in your hair." Jess reached out and pretended to take something; all the while pressing her hand.

Abigail's heart fluttered when he touched her hair. She ran her fingers through her hair and said, "Thank you Jess, whatever it was, must be gone. I hope you can come back soon."

"Don't worry, I will Abigail." He smiled at her, thanked her for the bread, mounted the horse, waved, and headed for home. Jess's heart was light, for he was falling for Abigail, and he knew that she was falling for him too. But, for now, there was nothing he could do about it. Perhaps he could visit her a little more often when he returned.   It would be a shame to lose such a lovely woman.

On his way home, Jess looked around at the beauty of the day. His heart was full, and his mind filled with all that God had provided. The loneliness seemed to be far away.

Chapter 8

It was the second week of October, and although the days were still warm, the nights were much colder. The leaves on the trees were brilliant with color, and when the wind blew, the leaves began to fall, forming a thick carpet of colorful hues.

Jiles David had walked out onto the porch with an egg basket in hand. He jumped off of the porch, and began kicking his way through the accumulated leaves. He ran to the barn and retrieved a rake, and soon the sound of the rake could be heard scratching along the ground as Jiles David put the leaves in a pile. Presently he began running and jumping in them; his laughter filling the air.

After a while his mother came out on the porch. She smiled and said, "Jiles David, that rake isn't the chicken coop, and those leaves aren't eggs. Now, you go gather the eggs; I can't cook breakfast without them. You can play in the leaves later."

"Yes mamma," he said. "I was only trying to have a little fun."

"I know, but I need the eggs, now get."

Jiles David retrieved the egg basket, and drug his feet through the leaves as he went to the chicken coop.

Back in the kitchen, Ruth waited for Jiles David to return. Suddenly he came rushing in the door and proclaimed, "Mamma," there is a big old possum out in the chicken coop! Do you want me to go get the gun mom?"

"No, Jiles David, I don't want you to get the gun. "Your dad or Jess is probably out in the barn, why don't you tell one of them."

Jiles David ran out the door and into the barn. Samuel was milking the cow, when Jiles David came dashing in. Jess was repairing a harness that had been broken, and the two men were discussing what needed to be done around the farm. They looked up when Jiles David came running in all out of breath. He didn't hesitate but blurted out. "Dad," there is a great big possum in the chicken coop, trying to eat the eggs, and mama won't let me get the gun! "What are we going to do?"

Samuel stopped milking, looked over at Jess and asked, "Jess," what do you think that should we do? Get some sweet potatoes out of the root cellar? I hear that possum and sweet potatoes are pretty good."

Jess smiled at Samuel's suggestion, and replied, "Oh, I don't know about that, Old George is my pet; I don't think I could eat him. Tell you what Jiles David, why don't we go to the chicken coop and see what he is up to." Jess picked up a gunny sack on the way out, and Samuel laughed and returned to the milking.

Jiles David asked, "Jess, are you going to shoot the possum?   Wasn't it going to kill the chickens and maybe even eat all the eggs?"

"Well, first of all, it isn't necessary to kill every animal; besides it would be a waste.
That old possum isn't really hurting anything, although it might kill a chicken or eat some of the eggs. What we will have to do is to catch Old George and turn him loose somewhere far off, and hope he won't return."

"Yes, but how are we going to catch Old George?"

"Oh, that's real easy Jiles David, come on I'll show you."

They entered the chicken coop and began looking for the possum. They found it in one of the many nesting boxes eating an egg. The possum, upon seeing them, grinned, showing his sharp teeth and began to hiss at them, Jiles David started to back up, but Jess made him stop.

"Here, you hold the gunny sack for me. Open it up

and I'll get Old George by the tail and then drop him inside." Jiles David did as he was told, and Jess deftly reached into the nesting box, grabbed the possum by the tail and held it up for Jiles David to see.

"Jess, aren't you afraid that George will bite you? Look at those sharp teeth!"

"No, I'm not afraid. He is playing possum now."

"What do you mean playing possum?"

"Jiles David, if a possum gets too scared he passes out. We call it playing possum. That is his way of protecting himself. He thinks that we will leave him alone and go away and not bother him." Jess dropped the possum into the sack, and tied it shut. Sure is a heavy possum, he must have eaten a hundred eggs."

Jess laughed and replied, "I hope not, we might want some breakfast ourselves. Now, why don't you finish gathering eggs, the egg basket is over there in the corner where you left it."

Jiles David got the basket and started to gather eggs again; being very careful to look into each nest, making sure that there wasn't another possum lurking inside the.

Jess took the possum to the barn, saddled up his horse and said, "Samuel I'm going to take this possum out into the woods, unless you want to eat him."

Samuel laughed, "Jiles David was excited about that possum wasn't he? And no, I don't want to eat it, I'm not that hungry; they are too greasy for me."

"Okay, I just wanted to make sure before I haul him off. I'll be back in a little while."

Jess tied the sack onto the back of the saddle, and made his way to the woods.

The entire time that the possum was in the sack, it didn't move a muscle. Sal could tell there was something alive was in the sack, and she didn't care for it at all. She began nickering, and lowering her head. Once or twice Jess had to rein her in, trying to stop her antics. He finally had to dismount. When he did this she settled down a little. Jess spoke to Sal, and rubbed her neck and ears, talking to her in soothing tones. After several minutes he remounted and continued on.

When Jess had reached the edge of the woods, he didn't hesitate, but plunged down a trail. He didn't turn the possum loose right away, because he wanted it away from the farm.

Jess was glad for the possum; it gave him a chance to ride. He continued down the dim trail, and made his way deeper into the trees.

It was early in the morning when he left the farm, and Jess decided there was plenty of time. The only thing he hadn't thought to bring was some food. He hadn't even brought water with him, but that didn't really matter, because there was always the creek to drink out of.

As Jess rode through the trees, he began to think about the abandoned Indian village and the burial mound. He decided to go over that way and have another look around.

Jess covered a good bit of ground until he found the trail that led in the right direction. He had been meandering around on purpose, enjoying every moment of the ride, and after about two hours in this manner, he emerged from the trail, and came out at the Indian village. He tethered Sal to a nearby bush, got the sack, walked over to the trees and turned the possum loose. The animal didn't waste any time, but waddled off into the woods and disappeared. Jess hoped that it didn't return to the farm; it was a harmless animal, and he didn't really want to kill it.

The Indian village seemed eerily silent. He tried to imagine what life had been like there.
Surely, Indian life must have been much like his own.
Mothers, fathers, and children, had trod the soil, going

about their lives, not knowing the change that would come.

Jess began to closely examine the area, looking for evidence of the Indians existence. He walked around, hoping to find something to take away with him. As Jess searched, he began thinking about Grey Wolf, and where he could be, and then something in the dirt caught his eye. Jess reached down, brushed away the loose dirt, and picked up a necklace of bear claws. It had evidently been lost in a struggle. He was surprised the necklace had survived this long. It made him wonder who it had belonged to. Such a prized possession must have been worn by a great warrior or perhaps a chief. He put the necklace in his coat pocket, to be examined later.

Jess continued the search, hoping to find more artifacts that would give insight into the Indian's lives.

After about another hour of exploration, he decided to return home. The Wilsons might begin to wonder what had happened to him.
Without further delay he saddled up, headed back down the trail and went home.

It was just about his lunch time when Jess rode up into the yard. He led Sal to the water trough, let her drink, and walked her back to the barn.

Jess removed his boots, and just as soon as he stepped inside, he saw Ruth working at the stove. He waited for her greeting, and sure enough, she turned and asked, "Hi Jess, did you wipe your feet?" Jess laughed and said, "Nope, I didn't. My boots were soiled, so I left them outside."

"Why, thanks Jess. I know you must be tired of me asking that same question, but my mamma drilled it into me, and it has become a habit. I hope you don't mind. I just want to make sure your house is in order. I wouldn't feel right if it wasn't."

Jess looked at Ruth and replied, "You are doing a

great job of looking after us, and no, Ruth, I don't mind at all. It reminds me of my mother."

Jess had finally overcome the uneasiness he felt when she insisted that they wipe their feet before entering the house. Ruth was only trying to keep everything in order; it was just her way of saying thank you.

"Ruth," Jess said, "where is Jiles David? I have something to show him."

"I'm not too sure, but he should be with Samuel. They will be here in a few minutes though, because lunch is about ready. Would you like a cup of coffee until they come in?"

"Sure," he replied. "I'm always ready for some coffee."

Ruth poured a cup and he sat down in the rocker by the hearth, and enjoyed its heady aroma. The fire crackled in the hearth, and its warmth began to make him sleepy, but he resisted dozing off, and just sipped his coffee.

Samuel and Jiles David came in, and they both said at once, "Yes we did."

"Okay you two," Ruth said. Don't forget that it's your lunch time. I might not be very generous when I spoon out the food."

"Yes mam," they returned, but continued laughing as they sat at the table.

Jess got up out of the rocker and joined them, refilling his cup as he went.

Samuel asked, "How did it go with George the possum Jess?"

"Oh he was glad to get out of that sack. I just hope he doesn't come back. Maybe he won't, I took him for a long ride. Speaking of a long ride," he intoned, "Do you know where I went this morning Jiles David? I went to an old Indian village in the woods. Let me show you what I found."

He pulled the necklace out of his pocket and handed it to him.

Jiles David gasped. "What is it? How did you find it? Did it belong to an Indian?"

Jess said, "Yes, I found it in the dirt at the old Indian village. I think it belonged to an important Indian. Why don't you try it on for size?"

Jiles David slipped it over his head and let it dangle around his neck. The look on his face was priceless. He was grinning from ear to ear.

"Just think, Samuel said, this might have belonged to a Chief. He probably wore it on the war path, and now you are wearing it."

Jiles David's face glowed with excitement as he fingered the claws of the necklace.

Ruth broke the spell by saying, "Ok", Jiles David, come back from the war path. Let Jess have the necklace back. It's time to eat." Jiles David looked disappointed, but took the necklace off and handed it back to Jess, who said, "Tell you what, how about if I let you look at it after lunch?" This pleased Jiles David and he vigorously shook his head.

Jess had been waiting to tell the Wilsons that he was planning a trip in the spring, or possibly in the summer, and didn't think he would find a more opportune time than now. The necklace he had found seemed to be as good a starting point as any, so, after they had eaten, he broached the subject. He and Samuel were sitting around the hearth, so, he handed him the necklace. "Samuel, I have been waiting for the right time to talk to you about something. Did I ever tell you about the Indian that I took in a while back? It was the winter before you came. I don't think I ever did."

Samuel looked at him in disbelief. Ruth stopped what she was doing, and came and stood by the hearth to listen to his tale.

When Jess had finished, Ruth asked, "Well, Jess, do you think any of the Indians will ever find their way back?   I mean, they are savages!"

"Ruth, Samuel, when I took Grey Wolf in, he was just a young man; filled with anger. When my parents were taken away from me, I was angry also, but God sent my neighbors and friends to help me. When I saw the anger in Grey Wolf, my heart was sorrowful for that young man. I couldn't help but have some compassion. He has gone now, looking for his family, and I hope he finds them. But there is one more thing I must tell you."

At this juncture of the story, Jess paused for a moment, and then began again, saying, "When Parson Walsh asked had me to take you in, I was very reluctant to do so. I had been alone since my family passed away, and I had a lot of resentment in me.

But, now I know that God had a plan for my life, and you have become a big part of it. You have, in a way, taken my parents place and given me the feel of having a family.

What I am about to tell you next might come as a surprise, but it is something that I feel I must do, and I think that Parson Walsh would approve."

This spring, or perhaps when the crops are all in, I plan on looking for Grey Wolf; to see if he will come back here.   This is where he belongs. I feel very strong about this, and I want you folks to help me pray about it. I have told the Springers what I intend to do, and they said that they would help with the farm work; just in case you folks find a place of your own."

Samuel said, "Jess I can feel conviction in your words. I think that is a very noble thing to do. I have never heard of anyone reaching out like that. You can depend on us to do all we can to help you, and our prayers are forth coming."

Ruth looked at Jess and said, "Jess, you are walking by faith, while all I could see was the bad in the Indians, but you have opened my eyes. I will indeed stand by you, come what may."

Jess felt very relieved by Ruth and Samuel's remarks, and thanked them for understanding, and said that he hadn't really come up with a plan of travel as yet, because he wanted to make sure the farm would be taken care of. He couldn't just up ride away. But now he thought that he could see his way clear.

Chapter 9

November came and went, and the harsh reality of winter was upon the land. The cold settled in, and snowfalls were frequent, but the weather was not severe. They struggled with cold, but managed to keep things going. Ruth kept the household without too many inconveniences. She even put a little rug just inside the door for the men to put their soiled boots on, and she had finally stopped telling them to wipe their feet.

Thanksgiving holiday had come and gone, and now it was getting close to Christmas, so Jess and Samuel decided to go on a turkey hunt. The day was cold to say the least, and they had bundled up against the chill. The men headed out across the field, and into the shelter of the woods. Here they tethered their horses and began their hunt. Jess went one direction and Samuel in another.

Samuel walked as quietly as possible in the fallen leaves until he found a likely spot, and then began calling for turkeys. The sound of his call echoed throughout the glens. He called a few times and stopped, and listened. Presently a turkey began to gobble. Samuel repeated the call, and the turkey answered him. Samuel grinned as he made ready to shoot. He sat very still for several minutes, and then called one more time. The turkey suddenly appeared a few yards right in front of him. He took careful aim and fired.

The turkey fell over. Samuel jumped up and retrieved the large bird. "Turkey dinner; he proclaimed out loud. He went back into his concealment and sat down, in case another turkey came. About an hour later, he heard Jess shoot his gun. "Two turkeys, I hope."

After a long while, he heard Jess making his way through the woods. When Samuel saw him, he said, "Jess, I don't know if Ruth will be happy or mad. Now there are two turkeys to cook. Well at least we won't starve." They walked back to the horses, hung the turkeys behind their saddles and headed for home.

As they rode across the field a cold wind began to blow, and then a few snowflakes started falling. It seemed that another round of snow was upon them, but it soon petered out and turned to sleet. Jess and Samuel urged their horses on, trying to get back to the house. The sleet stung them, and caused the horses to slip on the frozen ground. It was touch and go for a while, but they finally made it home without mishap. They rode to the barn, unsaddled the horses, dressed the turkeys, and hung the fan of feathers on the barn wall.

Jess and Samuel, having finished dressing the turkeys, took them to the kitchen. Ruth exclaimed. "Guys, what am I going to do with two turkeys? We can't possibly eat all of that meat; can we put one of them in storage?"

Jess replied, "Our intent is to smoke the turkeys, or I could give one to the Springers. That might be the thing to do. After all, Christmas is coming up."

Samuel and Ruth thought giving one of the turkeys to the Springers was a good idea. Ruth said, "Christmas is only three days from now, but it won't take long to smoke them. Their family is larger than ours. I'll bet they could use the extra meat."

Jess said that he would start a fire for the smoke house, and the birds could smoke until morning.

He went outside, gathered some kindling and hickory firewood, and then built a fire in the covered fire pit. Samuel brought the turkeys out, and hung them in the building. Then Jess soaked some of the wood in water, and put it on the flames. Soon smoke began to fill with aromatic smoke. Throughout the day the men added more wood to the fire to keep the smoke going. It helped to preserve the meat, and by morning, the turkeys would be ready for a Christmas dinner.

During the day, the weather shifted from sleet to snow. Jess and Samuel took turns adding wood to the fire, and despite the bad weather, the men managed to keep the fire burning. When it was night time, they would have to put enough wood on to make the fire last all night.

The next day, Jiles David was playing in the barn exploring its nooks and crannies. He had gotten tired of just sitting in the house doing nothing, so he had bundled up against the cold and went outside to play. As he explored at the back of the barn, he found an object that had been covered up with a tarp. He looked at it, trying to decide what it could be. His curiosity was aroused, and so he lifted one edge of the tarp and peeked in. He let out a gasp when he saw what the object was. He couldn't believe his eyes. It was beautiful. Jiles David lowered the tarp and dashed out and into the house. The men were sitting by the hearth, and Ruth was sitting with them knitting a sweater.

Ruth asked, "Jiles David what in the world are you up to? You look like you have seen a ghost."

He replied, "Mamma, you won't believe what is just found out in the barn!"

"Have you been snooping around in Jess's things?"

Jiles David said, "But Mamma, I was only playing. It was cold outside so I went into the barn to play. I wasn't hurting anything."

"I don't care what you were doing in the barn. You Know you shouldn't snoop around in someone else's things."

Samuel broke in and asked, "Jiles David, ok, what

could be in the barn that would get you so excited?"

Jess spoke up and said, "Samuel, I don't mean to interfere in your family business, but I know what got Jiles David so worked up." "Jiles David," "is what you found, covered?

Jiles David replied, "Yes it is. Boy, Jess, it was beautiful!"

Excitement could be seen on Jiles David's face. "Ruth, Samuel, don't be hard on him. I got excited the first time I saw it too."

Ruth spoke up and said, "I can't imagine what in the world has got him so worked up. What is out there in that barn?"

"Ruth, I'm going to show you what is out there, but you must stay in here and not look outside until I tell you to. I'm going to need Samuel and Jiles David's help with this."

Ruth could not imagine what was in the barn. She had been out there before, but hadn't seen anything out of the ordinary, only some tools, harnesses, and a shaving horse. Ruth just couldn't figure it out.

Jiles David smiled and said, "Mamma, in a minute, you will see why I go excited. It's just like Christmas!"

This little hint gave her a glimmer of what was hidden in the barn. She wasn't sure, but, she did have an idea.

She said, "Okay you guys, get on with it, or I'll go out and see for myself." They laughed at this, and went out to the barn.

Samuel asked, "Jess, what did Jiles David see? I haven't looked around at your belongings. But now I want to know what it is."

Jess said, "come on back here with me and I'll show you exactly what Jiles David found."

He went over to the tarp, and pulled it off.

"Well I'll be, Samuel said. "It's a sleigh, a beautiful sleigh. No wonder Jiles David got so excited. Why do you keep it covered up in here, you should be using it."

Jess answered, "My dad made this sleigh. We always went on great sleigh rides on the holidays. I want to preserve it, to honor my family, so I keep it covered up.

"Jess, we are your family now. Don't you think it's time it was used?" Don't let your loss direct your path. It is high time you let go of the hurt and start enjoying life again.

Why don't we all go for a sleigh ride? It would do us some good. Besides, when Ruth sees this sleigh, you are going to have a hard time keeping her out of it. Her mom and dad had one, and believe me they made good use of it."

Jess knew that Samuel's advice was very sound. It was high time he began thinking of himself. Jess didn't hesitate. "Samuel, I think that the sleigh will slide easily enough if we toss loose hay under the runners. When we get it close enough to the door we can hitch one of the sorrels to the sleigh. I have kept everything we need under the seat. It even has sleigh bells."

Jess and Samuel lifted up the front of the sleigh, and Jiles David tossed handfuls of hay underneath the runners. Then they moved a few things out of the way and began shoving the sleigh toward the front of the barn. Jess took one of the sorrels out of the stall and began hitching it to the sleigh. Soon the bells on the harness were jingling. Samuel opened the barn door, and Jess and Jiles David drove the sleigh to the house. Ruth came out onto the porch. "Why, what a wonderful Sleigh! It reminds me of our own sleigh back home. It makes me homesick." Tears began filling her eyes, and she wiped them on her sleeve and said, "Of course, you have to take me for a ride." Samuel helped Ruth get in the sleigh and when they all settled down, Jess said,

"Giddy up there Kit!" The horse leaned into the harness, and began pulling the sleigh up the lane and to the road. The runners made a swishing sound, and the bells jingled as they went. Jiles David smiled and laughed. It wasn't long before Ruth started singing Jingle Bells, and they all joined in; their voices rang loud and clear in the cold winter atmosphere.

When they reached the end of the lane, Jess asked, "Okay folks, what do you think? Shall we go a little bit farther? Or are you too cold?"

Jiles David piped up, "I'm not cold Jess. I want to keep going, this is fun!"

"Well then, if everyone agrees, shall we go?"

Ruth and Samuel were beaming down at Jiles David and said that a longer ride would be nice. So Jess urged the horse on, and they came out of the lane and went gliding down the road.

After about half an hour of sleighing, Jiles David said, "Dad, my feet are getting cold, and my hands are about frozen." Ruth put her arms around him, and tried to get him warm.

Samuel said, "Jess we have a boy back here that is frozen, I guess we had better get him home so he can thaw out."

Jess replied, "It is brisk out here; perhaps we had better head for home." Jess turned the sleigh around and headed back.

When they got back to the house, Samuel picked Jiles David up and took him straight to the hearth. He looked at him and asked, "Did you have a good time Jiles David?"

"I sure did. Can we do that tomorrow?"

Samuel laughed and replied. "You will just get cold again."

Jiles David said, "I'll thaw out."

When Ruth went into the house, she put on a pot of coffee, and made Jiles David a cup of hot tea. The sweet liquid warmed his insides, and it wasn't very long before he was taking his coat off.

Jess came in the house and said, "Since the horse is still hooked to the sleigh, I think I will take the turkey to the Springers. The weather isn't threatening, and it would do me good to visit and wish them Merry Christmas. And, Samuel, you are right about the sleigh. It needs to be used. My parents would want it that way."

Ruth said, "Jess, I know we could never take the place of your family, but we do want you to know that we are here for you, and are willing to do whatever it takes to help."

Jess was touched by their sincerity. He knew that God had sent the Wilsons to help. He was sure there would be lonely times, but at least now he had someone that would help. The sleigh ride had been great fun, and It felt as if his own family had been riding. It brought him hope for the future.

After getting warm by the fire, he bundled up again, went to the smoke house, and took down one of the turkeys, placed it in a gunny sack, put it in the sleigh, and headed up the lane again.

Chapter 10

The five mile ride to the Springers was a cold one. When Jess finally pulled into their lane, he was shivering all over. The last few yards to their house seemed the longest. When he pulled in yard, Jess was greeted by the entire family. Marta said, "Jess we heard you clear down the lane. I thought Santa Clause was here. I'm glad to see you driving the sleigh. I still remember your mom and dad coming to take us rides. Those were fun times. Come on in the house before you freeze."

Jess retrieved the turkey and said to her, "Marta, Santa Clause did come early; I have a present for you."

"Well, Jess, I can't imagine what it could be. Come over by the fire and get warmed up while I fix you something to drink."

Jess put the turkey on the table and sat by the fireplace. It wasn't very long until the heat began penetrating his bones. Abigail brought him the coffee. Jess smiled at her and said, "Why, thank you, this should warm me up."

Abigail was about to say something, but her dad asked, "Jess, how are things going at the farm? Is everything still working out? Did you tell the Wilsons you would be leaving for a while?"

"Yes, I did tell them, and they were okay with it. They have been a great to me.

About this time, Marta let out a gasp and proclaimed. "Charles, Jess brought a turkey! Come and look at how big it is."

Charles went to the table to see the bird and replied. "Jess, what a nice turkey this is! Now I won't have to go hunt for one."

Charles looked at the big turkey and said, "Ruth, this turkey has been in a smoker. It should have a good rich hickory flavor.

"Samuel got one too, and we thought we would share with your family for Christmas."

Ruth was grateful for the generosity, and said, "Jess, before you go home, I'm going to give you a jar of jam and a loaf of my bread for your kindness; it's the least we could do."

Abigail broke in on the conversation, and asked, "Jess, can I look at your sleigh? Was it a fun ride?"

Jess didn't hesitate, but replied, "Yes, it was a real fun ride. As matter of fact, I took the Wilsons on a ride before I came over. It was cold, but worth it. Would you like to take a ride Abigail?"

"Why, I sure would. Thank you for asking Jess. I would love to." They went outside and found Matthew and Caleb admiring the sleigh.

Mathew asked, "Jess can I get in and go for a ride?

"Why, of course you can. Let's go."
Matthew got in the sleigh and said, "come on everybody, we are going for a sleigh ride."

Caleb looked at Jess and shook his head.
Jess just smiled and said,   "We better get in before Matthew leaves without us." They all laughed at this and got in the sleigh.

There was only room for four people, so Charles and Marta were left standing on the porch as they drove away. Jess called back to them, "Your turn is next." Charles and Marta smiled, waved, and then went back into the warmth of the house.

As the sleigh glided down the long lane, Abigail remarked about how cold it was. Jess looked at her and replied, "Why don't you move over a little? That might help you stay warm."

"Careful, you two; don't get to comfortable up there."

Matthew starting laughing and asked, "Are you that

cold Abigail?" I'm hardly cold at all."

"Yes, I'm freezing! Jess is only trying to help keep me warm."

As soon as the words were out of Abigail's mouth she regretted it, and started moving away, but Jess reached over and pulled her to his side.

He said, "Don't pay any attention to them Abigail; I noticed that they are huddling close together trying to stay warm."

Abigail started laughing, moved a little bit closer to Jess, saying, "This is much better. I'm not quite as cold now."

Jess looked at Abigail, smiled at her and replied, "I'm not quite as cold either Abigail."

The bells on the harness jingled as the sorrel pulled the sleigh. Their laughter floated on the cold air as they slid up the lane. They were having a wonderful time in the snow.

When they got back from the ride, they went into the house and to the hearth trying to absorb its radiant heat. Jess only lingered a while, and said that he had better start for home. Charles and Ruth had taken a sleigh ride while everyone else was getting warm. When they got back Ruth proclaimed, "That was so much fun, but it is too cold to stay out for very long."

Charles asked, "Where is that hot coffee?

Before Jess left, he said, "I might not get to see you for a while, but I hope you have a very Merry Christmas. Drop around sometime if you get the chance. I'm sure the Wilsons would like to see you." They thanked Jess for the turkey, and said that they would be sure to drop by for a visit sometime.

Abigail gave Jess his jam and bread, and thanked him for the ride. She said. "Jess that was the most fun I've had in a long time. I would like to do that again."

Jess saw the warmth in her eyes, and it made his heart skip a beat. "Why of course I'll take you for a ride if we happen to get a warmer day. I just might show up."

Abigail smiled and said, I hope so Jess, I would like that very much."

Jess knew that Abigail cared for him, and he didn't really want to leave, but responsibility of the farm was calling. He said, "Abigail I'll come to see you before long." Jess went out in the cold and got into the sleigh.

Abigail and Matthew followed Jess outside, and Matthew said, "I wish we had a sleigh.

As Jess pulled away, he turned and said, "Merry Christmas. Keep an eye out for that warm day."

"What did he mean Abigail is Jess going to come back?"

"Oh, you never can tell Matthew, it could be." They watched as the sleigh started up the lane and listened to the jingling of the bells, until the cold forced them back inside.

Jess felt satisfied. He knew that his life was going to change. It was just a matter of time. The more he was around Abigail, the more he saw good in her. He admired her, and the admiration was turning into affection. He almost wished he hadn't made plans to leave, but he couldn't back out now. He had laid his plans, and felt obligated to Grey Wolf. His journey could lead anywhere, but he was confident everything would turn out alright.

The intense cold was getting to Jess, and he had to rub his hands and legs to keep the circulation. The five miles home seemed like ten. The sleigh swished through the snow, and the breath from the sorrel turned into small clouds of white vaper;
some of it even crystalized on the horse's nostrils. Jess wasn't faring much better, and he was glad when

he was able to turn the sleigh into the lane, and finally make it back to the barn.

Jess unhitched the sorrel from the sleigh, put the horse into a stall, forked in some hay, and gave it a bucket of grain. The horse had done well, fighting against the cold. Jess was about frozen and hurried into the house and went straight to the hearth. Samuel poured him a hot cup of coffee, proclaiming, "Jess, it's about time you came in. We were getting worried about you. We were glad to hear the sleigh coming down the lane."

"Jess replied, "Yes, it is so cold out there, but I made back without freezing to death. The Springers were glad to get the turkey. The timing was perfect. Charles said that he was going hunting tomorrow, but that we saved him a trip."

Ruth asked, "Are you hungry Jess? I have some leftovers if you want them. I have put on a pot of beans, but they won't be ready until this afternoon."

"I wouldn't refuse left overs. Abigail sent a jar of jam and some bread with me. That should go good with leftovers."

The next day or two was a very busy time for Ruth. She was preparing for Christmas, and as she worked in the kitchen, her thoughts turned to her family and she wished to see them. There hadn't been an answer to the letter, but knew that it might take a year for it to get to its destination, because the letter would have to be passed from hand to hand until it got delivered. It would have been nice to have heard from her family, but there was nothing to be done but wait. Ruth believed that sooner or later some news would come from them. She was just glad to have a roof over her head.

Christmas came on the back of a blustery snow storm, the wind driving the wet snow before it. It was intensely cold, and snow began to pile in great heaps.

Ropes had to be tied from the house, and barn, and chicken coop. The wind- blown snow made it almost impossible to see. If anyone got lost, it wasn't likely that they would find their way back to the house again. So it was, that Jess and the Wilsons were pretty much prisoners. They didn't go outside unless they absolutely had to. There was firewood under the shelter of the porch roof, but it was still challenging to get it. Feeding and watering the animals was almost impossible, but, it had to be done anyway, so Jess and Samuel went together to do the necessary chores, to insure that they made it back to the house safe and sound.

Ruth had prepared the Christmas dinner despite the bad weather, so they sat down to enjoy the meal. Samuel said grace, thanking the Lord for keeping them all safe from the storm, and for providing food. They partook of the meal, talking in hushed conversation as they listened to the howling wind pushing against the house.

It was late in the evening, when the wind died down. The sun was setting, and twilight descended. Jess went to the front door, and looked outside. The snow had stopped falling and the landscape looked strange in the dim light. The clouds still lingered, but there were a few places in the clouds where the sky was shining through. It looked as if the storm had finally blowing out.   It was still intensely cold, but they had endured the worst of the storm.

Christmas day hadn't exactly been ornate, because the weather had been severe. There wasn't even a Christmas tree, but they were glad to be blessed with what they had.

Ruth hung stockings on the mantle, and there was homemade candy in each one. She handed out the stockings after the meal. Jiles David eagerly looked in his stocking to see what surprise was hidden there.

Ruth had knitted mittens for Jiles David and the men, and then Jiles David pulled out a small bundle of candy, and a wooden top Samuel had made for him. He didn't waste any time, but eagerly indulged in the sweets.

Ruth had put some of the candy in her own stocking to be able to celebrate with the others, and Samuel had carved her a small bird to remind her of spring. It was a festive time despite the absence of a Christmas tree. The group then sat around the hearth and began to sing Christmas carols to celebrate.

Chapter 11

Jess and Samuel were doing the morning chores; dim light was just beginning to streak across the blue cloudless sky, and a rooster started crowing. Jess stopped what he was doing, and just stood still a moment listening, and after a few moments remarked, "Samuel, do you feel the change in the air? It won't be all that long before the geese fly over and it will be planting time again. I'll be glad when spring gets here."

"Well, Jess, I'm just as tired of the cold weather as you are. Spring will get here, but not soon enough for me either."

Jiles David came out on the porch and proclaimed, "Mamma said to come get some breakfast." He then ran back into the house and to the warmth of the fire. Old Man winters grip was still harsh, and things would remain that way until the March wind began to blow.

"I don't know about you Jess, but I'm not about to miss a hot meal. I'm starved. Let's go eat." Samuel picked up the milk pail and he and Jess went in to breakfast.

With the arrival of the much awaited spring thaw, and the diminishing of the cold winter days, the land was transformed. The first spring flowers began to appear and it wasn't long before buds appeared on the trees. Jess was glad to see spring's arrival. Not only did it mean that it wouldn't be long before the crops would be planted, but also by the summer, he could be on his way westward. He would stay until the crops were in the ground, and then it would be up to Samuel and Ruth to tend to things until he returned. The Wilsons had been a Godsend. They had at shown up just on time. Otherwise, he wouldn't have been going on his journey.

The day of Jesse's departure was a very pleasant one and he had gone outside to saddle his horse. The saddle bags were filled with such things that he needed for the trip, and before he started packing, Jess had gone into his parent's bedroom, and had carefully chosen one of his mother's hair combs as a present for Abigail. He wanted to give it to her as a promise that he would be coming back. He then secured his bedroll and tent behind the saddle. His preparations had been carefully made, and he was ready to go. Sal was quite anxious, and she would impatiently stomped her feet as Jess worked around her.

When he went back in the house, Samuel, Ruth, and Jiles David were there to see him off. Ruth had prepared a sack of food for his lunch, and Jiles David spoke up and asked, "Jess, do you need someone to go with you, just in case you need help with Sal?"

"Jiles David, that was nice of you to offer, but you know what? What I really need is for someone to look after my chickens, and I don't know anyone else who does a better job than you. Would you mind taking care of them for me until I get back?"

Jiles David smiled and replied, "Of course Jess. If that's what you would like me to do."

Ruth began to voice her concern about his leaving, but Samuel said, "Now, Ruth, Jess knows what he is doing; he will be just fine.

When Jess went on the road, he didn't immediately ride to the Springers house, but just sat and looked around at what he was leaving behind. It seemed a little strange to be embarking on such a journey. He did have some doubts as to the outcome. What if he was unable to find Grey Wolf? And if he did find him, there was no guarantee that he would come back. The realization that there were unknowns involved, played heavy on his mind.

He had gone over everything he could think of many times, and was confident of his abilities to make the trip. It was just a matter of not get tangled up with the wrong crowd.

The five mile ride to the Springers went by quickly enough, and before he knew it, he was stopping in front of their house.

He dismounted and walked Sal to the watering trough and let her drink. Charles, who had heard Jess coming, was standing in the barn door and called out, "Well, look who came over to help with all the chores." His lighthearted greeting made Jess laugh. He replied, "Charles, I didn't come away over here to work. I just came for Marta's cooking. She is one of the best cooks around."

They continued in this lighthearted banter until Marta came out on the porch and invited Jess in, saying, "Jess, don't pay any attention to Charles, he will put a pitchfork or shovel in your hand if you don't watch him."

Jess and Charles made their way into the house and sat down at the table. Marta said "Help yourself; to breakfast, I have got more chores than I can handle." Then she went to the door and called out, "Matthew, where are you with that firewood? I've got laundry to do."

Matthew came from around the backside of the house with an arm load of dry twigs. He said, "I heard ya calling, I was just gathering twigs to get the fire started."

"Well, alright, we will start the laundry as soon as the kettle is filled and the fire is hot enough."

"Okay mom, I filled the kettle a little while ago, and I have full buckets of water in case you need it mamma."

"Why, Matthew, she said, you're on top of things this morning aren't you. When you get the fire going,

I'll have some bread and jam waiting for you.

Matthew replied, "Yea, I thought that was his horse. I'll be in as soon as I get the fire going."

Matthew began to build the fire, and it wasn't long before he had a fire going under the kettle of water. Matthew watched it for a moment or two, and then went to the house.

As he entered the kitchen, he was greeted with, "Hey, Matthew, what are you trying do, starting a laundry service?"

"No, I'm just helping mom and Abigail; out laundry is woman's work."

Marta gave him a stern look and replied, "Careful there, young man, I'll put an apron on you!" Everyone laughed at her remark, and Matthew sat down at the table.

Abigail came out of one of the rooms with a basket load of clothes to be washed. She sat them by the door and said, "Hello, Jess, what brings you out this way?"

Jess felt his heart skip a beat at the sight of Abigail. He almost said, why, Abigail, you, of course, but thought better of it. Instead he said, "I came over for a good meal. I thought if I looked hungry, I'd get fed some of Marta's biscuits and gravy."

Abigail replied, "Well, Jess, I'll have you to know that I cooked breakfast today.

Jess looked at her and said, "Abigail, your mother taught you very well, that is one of the best breakfasts I ever had."

Abigail just shook her head, and replied, "I don't know Jess, mom's biscuits and gravy seems much better than mine."

"Charles spoke up and remarked, "At least it wasn't burnt sacrifice like the last time you made breakfast. We had to open the windows and doors to let the smoke out."

Matthew started laughing and said, "Yea, Abigail just about caught the house on fire!"

Just then Caleb came in from the field and asked, "What is so funny?"

Abigail said, "Oh, Caleb, they are making fun because I burnt the breakfast one time."

"I remember. I thought the house was on fire, the smoke was so thick!"

"Okay, if you are going to pick on me, I'll bring up a few things I know that mom and dad don't." Abigail gave Matthew and Caleb a smug look, winked at Jess and said, "I know how to put them in their place Jess. I've got lots of stuff written down, and I'll use it."

Matthew and Caleb said, "Okay, okay, we quit."

Charles asked, "Say, where do you keep that book on them, we want to see what you are talking about." Everyone laughed, and Marta asked, "If you are finished poking fun at Abigail, you can stop now. She has to help with the laundry. With that, Abigail and Marta got the laundry basket, and went outside to start their chore.

Jess and Charles went out on the porch, while Caleb and Matthew went about their work. Jess took this opportunity to explain his visit. He cleared his throat and started with, "Charles, do you remember me saying I would be taking a trip? Well, I have talked to the Wilsons about it, and they are willing to stay as long as they can. I was wondering if you are still going to check on the farm while I am gone."

"Yes, I remember our conversation, and of course we will check on things for you. And if the Wilsons decide to move on before you get back, we will take over as best we can. There is one thing I think you should consider though. Has it occurred to you that Abigail really cares for you? And it's not just Abigail. Marta and I care about you also Jess.

Jess felt a lump rise up in his throat when he heard

this from Charles. He felt a twinge of guilt, but had already made arrangements to leave, so he said, "Charles, what you just said means a lot to me. I know that I am taking a chance on this, but I really want to see it through. I think it is something that my dad would have done, had he been in the same situation."

"Jess," Charles replied, "I won't influence you any further, you are your own man, but I thought that I had to try anyway. We will be praying that you will have a safe return. I do think that you should speak to Abigail, if you have any feelings for her. You do know that there other men around that like her don't you? Marta and I have been observing, and we really believe that Abigail couldn't do any better than you Jess."

Jess didn't know what to say. He did have feelings for Abigail, but he hadn't expected Charles to urge him on. He grew silent for a few moments, trying to gather his thoughts. He finally asked, "So, what you are saying is that you would like for me to court Abigail?"

"Well, Jess, if you put it that way, I guess that is what I mean. Marta and I have been discussing this for a while, and as I said, we have watched, and We would never have to worry about our daughter with you. We really don't want to lose you. You belong in this family, but of course it is up to you."

"Charles, I have feelings for Abigail, she is a fine woman, and I will talk to her before I leave. I am headed out West today. I know that might sound a little bit strange to you, but it is something I feel I must do. We took Grey Wolf's family's land away from them. I just want to try and do something to make up for it. I know I may never find him, but I must try. I'll do my best to be back by the end of summer.

Charles thought he might be making a big mistake

by leaving, but he held his peace. Jess was a man and he knew his own mind.   "Jess, I hope all goes well, and while you are gone we will look after your farm. Just watch your back trail; there are a lot of bad men out there looking for an opportunity.

"I have been thinking about that Charles, and I'll take precautions. I have my rifle, and pistol, and I know how to use them."

Abigail came back inside just then, and Charles excused himself. Jess took this as a sign to speak to her, and he began with, "Abigail, I'm getting ready to leave, and I just wanted to tell you good bye. I told your dad that I would be back by summers end.

Jess began to get just a little nervous and started pacing back and forth. Once or twice he stopped to look out of the window trying to find the right words to say.

Abigail could feel Jesse's nervous energy, and knew that he had something important on his mind. She finally cleared her throat and said, "Jess, I hate to see you go. Are you sure you want to leave? Isn't there anything I can say that would persuade not to leave?" Abigail walked up to him and put her hand on his arm. Her touch sent a thrill through him, but he didn't say anything for a moment. Jess was feeling foolish. Here was a very beautiful woman practically begging him to stay, but he had already made up his mind to leave; he couldn't back out now. He waited a moment than said, "Abigail, I know I haven't come to see you often enough, and believe me, I'm really sorry for that. I wouldn't blame you if you didn't want to see me again, but I really wanted to talk to you before I leave. I have something for you. I want you to know how much I care. I think you are beautiful, and I count myself very lucky that you want me to stay.
I don't always l et my feelings show, but I care about you. I have talked with your dad, and have permission

to court you if you will allow it."

Abigail's heart skipped a beat, and she paused to catch her breath; then she replied, "Jess I would be honored. He looked into her blue eyes, took her hand and embraced her.

Jess produced his mother's hair comb and gave it to her and said, "Abigail, this was my mother's, and I would like for you to have it as a promise that I will return."

Abigail felt a warm glow begin to rise in her heart when Jess gave her the hair comb. She replied, "Oh, Jess, how sweet of you to give me something that belonged to her. I will cherish it always. I don't know what else to say, except that I love you and I am holding you to your promise to return to me."

Jess smiled, "Abigail, of course you know it is going to be difficult for me to leave. I have a long way to go, and it could take me longer than I think. You will wait for me won't you?"

"Oh, yes, I certainly will wait for you Jess. I have waited this long, I think can wait some more."

Jess smiled and replied, "I didn't think I would ever find someone to love. I figured I would always be alone. God had you there for me. I just didn't know it. I'm sorry it took me so long to realize it."

Abigail, reached out to Jess, and touched him. "Jess I always wondered if the right one would come along. I have had suiters come visit, but I knew that they weren't right for me. When you dropped by the first time, I had an inkling that you could be the one, and I knew it for sure when you kissed me at the shucking bee. I have been waiting for you to see it for yourself. I'm so glad that you did. I fell in love with you a long time ago."

"I love you too Abigail. I'm glad that you waited for me. I have had a hard time getting past the loss of my family. I just couldn't get over the pain, but it is going to be alright. Abigail reached up and put her hands on his face and gave him a tender kiss.

Chapter 12

As Jess made his way westward, and after having ridden two or three hours, he stopped to rest the horse and let her drink in a nearby stream. It was about noon, so he dismounted and decided to eat the lunch that Abigail had prepared for him. She had placed half a loaf of bread in his pouch, along with some fried bacon. He ate this with pleasure, because it came from her hands, and he smiled at the prospect of her becoming his wife.

Jess stayed by the stream for only a little while because he wanted to hasten his search for Grey Wolf. He was a little unsure of the exact direction he should go, but, from what he had heard about the Shawnee's removal, the Indians had been taken into Missouri, or even Kansas. They had been removed around 1826 or perhaps 1827. He was unsure of the exact date, but it was around the time that his family died. Jess had been so distraught over their passing, that he hadn't given the Indians removal a thought at the time. Now, however, it had become a priority to him, and he wanted to make the effort to find Grey Wolf. If he could find him, and persuade him to return, his trip would be worthwhile; if not, at least his conscious would be clear.

Jess had followed the road until it turned north. He didn't know where it went for sure, but he didn't think north was the direction to go in, so he found a trail headed west.

Jess took his time as he ride down the long winding trail, taking note of landmarks. At one point the trail had been widened, and he began seeing some land cleared of trees. The land was being farmed, or in the process of being farmed. Riding up a rather steep incline, Jess came upon a log cabin. It was just a small place, but well used. After being on the trail most of the day, Jess decided to rest Sal. He followed the trail up to the cabin, and before dismounting, he cried out, "Hello the house. Is there anyone at home?" Presently the door opened, and a wizened old woman came out.

She looked Jess and his horse over, and said, "How do, what brings you to this neck of the woods? Get on down offin your horse and set a spell. We don't get much company out this-a-way. Where ya headed, where did ya come from? Do ya have any folks out-an-about?"

Jess only smiled at her, and answered, "Hi mam, my name is Jess Fulmer, and I'm from over in Licking County."

The old woman walked to the far end of the porch, as if thinking over what Jess had said, she walked back, looked Jess up and down then said, "Waal, I heard of it.   My family is from West Verginy. We moved in here a few years back. We lost a child or two along the way. Life sure has been hard, but the Lord has been good to us anyway. Would ya like a cup of coffee?   My man has set out after a cow or two; don't expect him back till dark. I'll get a cup." With that the old woman went in the house. Jess just stood where he was until the woman came out of the house with a cup of coffee in one hand, and a plate of biscuits in the other. She said, "I can't stand to see a young man go without some grub. Come on up here on the porch and set a spell." Jess readily complied, and sat down in a rocker across from the woman. She sat the plate of biscuits on a stump that had been made into a small table and said, "Son, don't be bashful, but just dig right on in. My name is Maggie, Maggie Noble. My husband's name is Jedidiah."   After Maggie had said her piece, she grew quiet.

Between them they just about finished off the biscuits. Jess drained his coffee cup, set it aside and said, "Mrs. Noble, thank you so very much for the coffee and biscuits. I have come a long way and needed a rest."

Maggie asked, "Where are ya headed?"

Jess didn't hesitate, but replied, "Well, I am trying to find out in which direction the Shawnee Indians went, when the government relocated them. I know that they came this way from the stories I've heard, but I'm not all that sure."

Maggie didn't say anything for a moment, but when she did, she looked into Jess's eyes and said, "Them Indians weren't nothing but a bunch of cut throat murderers and thieves! They killed my two sons, and ran off with our horses! That was a long time ago, and it took me a spell to find fergiveness in my heart. If we don't forgive folks, the Lord won't forgive us. Do ya know when I was able to fergive them? It was the day that they came through on their way to a new reservation. They were the most bedraggled, sorry lookin bunch of people I ever came across. Their heads hung down, and they looked exhausted and ruined. The Lord spoke to my heart, and I fergave them then and there." Jess could see tears welling up in Maggie's eyes as she told her story.

Maggie spoke of how her two boys had gone out to hunt deer. "They had been gone only an hour or two, when we heard shots. I thought that they both had shot something, but when they didn't come home we began to worry about them. My husband decided to go and look for them, and he found em alright. They had been tortured, and then scalped by the Indians. He wouldn't let me see them. They are buried side by side on that small hill over yonder. We never did find out which Indians did it, and I don't expect we ever will. I've made peace with God.

Jess consoled Maggie as best he could, and told her how he had lost his family to sickness, that it had taken him a long time to overcome his grief. Then he related how he had started on his journey to find Grey Wolf. He said, "I don't know if I will ever find him or not. But this one thing I know. It is in my heart to do this, and I must try. One way or the other I will succeed. There is no failure in trying."

Jess visited with Maggie an hour or two then said that he had better be on his way. She fixed him a small lunch, and wished him well and said. "Son, you be careful who you talk to, and don't trust anyone you meet on the road, and be on guard. If you come back this way, stop in and I'll feed you. God bless you with a safe journey."

Jess thanked Maggie, mounted his horse, and once again hit the trail through the trees.

The day was advancing into late evening when Jess decided that he had better make a camp before sunset. He got off the trail, and rode back into a denser part of the woods so his camp couldn't be seen. There was a stream close by, and so Jess set up his tent and built his fire up under the low hanging limbs of a tree, so that the smoke would be dissipated. When everything was in order, he settled down for the night and ate some food Maggie had provided for him.

As the sun set and dusk began settling down around the camp, sounds of eventide began filling the air. The glow from his fire reflected off of the trees and brush, casting dancing shadows all around. He hoped that the fire couldn't be seen from the trail, but he needn't have worried, for the brush was thick enough to hide it from view.

The next morning Jess was awakened by raindrops hitting his tent. He looked outside, and it was just getting daylight.

There were streaks of light above the tree tops; so, Jess got out and managed to get a fire started. Soon the coffee was ready, and he fried a little bacon, and ate it with one of Maggie's left over biscuits.

The rain shower didn't increase in volume, but just sprinkled down in small drops, and it didn't look like it would hinder his travel very much, and after packing the tent and bedroll away, he tidied up around the camp, put the fire out, mounted Sal, and headed down the trail.

Jess traveled for most of the day without having seen anyone, and concluded that he must have missed the trail somewhere, but then he remembered that several years had passed since the Indians had been that way. It was likely that all traces of their passing had been erased by time. As Jess pondered upon this, Sal suddenly raised her ears. Jess heeded the horses warning, and quickly got off of the trail, and rode into the thick brush. It wasn't long before he heard the sound of horses. Jess sat very still and waited.

It wasn't very long before a large group of rough looking riders came around a bend in the trail. He watched as they approached the point where he had entered the woods. They didn't stop to look around, but went on by. The riders didn't seem to be in any kind of a hurry at all, and he caught snatches of their conversations as they rode. From what he had heard, they must have been some cow pokes. He waited until they had passed by and then went back out onto the trail and started again.

Along about evening, Jess saw someone walking. Instead of getting off of the trail, he advanced until he caught up with whoever it was.

The person heard Jess coming and turned around to look at him. It was a small man, and he had the look of a farmer about him, and seemed worse for the wear. His clothes were a bit ragged, and he had a stern look about him, but when Jess spoke to him, the man's face lit up. He said. "How do stranger. What brings you to these parts?"

Jess was taken off guard. From the first look of the man, he had expected a rebuke. He answered, "Well sir, this may sound a bit strange, but I am looking for an Indian.

"I'll be jigged. If that don't beat all; why there were so many Indians that came by here that you could have stirred em with a stick. I really felt sorry for them. Some were bare foot, and they were the most unlikely bunch of folks I ever laid my eyes on.
I do believe they were headed for Missouri, or Kansas. Any way, they passed through quite a while back."

Jess conversed with the man for a while longer, and decided that he had better get a move on and start looking for a good place to camp. He thanked the man and mentioned that he was looking for a place to rest his horse before dark.   The man said, "Son, me and my brother got burnt out a while back, and we have been staying down in the valley over yonder way. It ain't much to look at, but you are more than welcome to spend the night with us; if you've a mind to. There is a crick close by, and you can rest your horse there."

"I'm sorry real to hear about your cabin."

"Oh, it was just one of those things. The chimney caught on fire and try as we might, we just couldn't put it out. My brother and I managed to get some of our belongings out, but the rest of it burnt up. We were lucky to get out alive; now we are living in a cave of sorts. We manage, but it ain't easy."
Jess said, "I'm Jess Fulmer, I'm sorry you and your brother. It must be difficult living in a cave."

"Oh, you don't have to feel sorry for us. The good Lord kept us alive. Things will get better. We still have the barn and the chicken coop. We were going to live in the barn, but the cave is in better shape than it is. By the way, I'm Seth Hooper. My brother's name is Sy. I'm headed home, why don't you come along with me and you can get settled in." Jess didn't hesitate but agreed to follow him, although he did wonder what he was getting himself into.

Seth walked down the trail quite a little ways and then took a dim path through the trees and into a hollow. He went a short ways on this path and then stopped in front of an overhanging ledge. Jess had never seen a shelter quite like it before. Seth and Sy had gathered corn shocks, bound them together, and made a wall out of them. It closed in the front of the overhang. They had fashioned a door of sorts, out of tree limbs and covered it with evergreens. They did their cooking on a raised shelf in a part of the overhang. Jess was impressed by what they had built; using only those things that came to hand.

It was about dusk when Sy Hooper came in from the woods. He carried two rabbits in his hand. As soon as he saw Jess, he asked, "Where did you drop in from? You're not from around these parts."

Seth said, "Now Sy, don't get all riled up. This is Jess Fulmer, from up around Licking County. I invited him to stay. He was looking for a place to hang his hat."

Sy looked Jess over and said, "Well, if it's okay with Seth, it's okay with me. We hain't got a whole lot of food to eat, but I guess I don't mind sharin with you. Food gets a little scarce sometimes."

Jess thanked Sy and said, "If you are willing to share with me, the least I can do is to share too.
He went to his saddle bags and got out the biscuits that Maggie had sent along with him.

Sy proclaimed, "Well, glory be, biscuits! We'll have a feast now boys!" Sy started cleaning the rabbits and

Seth soon had a hot fire going. They put the rabbits on sticks, and it wasn't too long before the aroma of fried rabbit filled the air.

Jess learned a little bit more about the Hooper brothers. It seemed that they had come into that part of the country a few years back. The brothers had been just like everyone else. They had come west looking for adventure and decided to stay. The two men didn't have any family to speak of, and never got married. Everything was going fine until the fire. Now they had to rebuild and start all over. They had one milk cow, some chickens and an old mule. It was their first winter in the shelter, but they had plenty of fire wood, and supplemented their meals with wild game, milk and eggs. They managed a small garden, and it was just enough to help supply their needs.

The whole time Jess was with Seth and Sy, he never did hear them complain about their situation. They just seemed to roll with the punches and kept going. Jess recognized the pioneer spirit in them. It was what had built the country. It was the same spirit that his father and mother had, and he had that spirit too. The next day Jess said goodbye to Seth and Sy and rode up out of the hollow.

Chapter 13

Two weeks later Jess was on the bank of the Ohio River. He just sat on his horse and looked down onto the flow. There was a ferry a few yards away, and so he inquired about the Indians. The man who ran the ferry was a crude looking person. His grey hair was long and quite unkempt, and when Jess asked him about the Indians, he began to curse, telling Jess, "Only an ignorant fool would go chasing after a bunch of thievin cut throat Indians."

Jess wasn't surprised by his rudeness, for most folks didn't have any use for Indians. He didn't inquire further, but just asked if he could be ferried across. The man said, "Son, it ain't none of my cotton pickin business, but them Indians didn't ford here. The Govment put them on rafts to Missouri and sent them on their way, and good riddance to em!" With that the man turned away without uttering another word.

Jess sat on his horse for a few moments trying to make up his mind. At least now he knew what direction the Indians went. Now all he had to do was to get across the river.

Jess had about decided to ride on when a man and a woman riding a buckboard came along. He waited for them to catch up. When they did, he waved his hat at them.

The man stopped the buckboard and said, "Howdy, you look kinda lost, what can I do for ya?"

Jess replied, "Well, just to be honest with you, I wanted to ferry across the river, but that gentleman over there wasn't very obliging."

The man reached out his hand and said, "Glad to help if I can; I'm Julies Parker, and this is my wife Ann. We were just headed to town. You are welcome to go with us. You will have to excuse Rufus he wakes up grumpy and goes to bed the same way. Never has a good thing to say. He is a misery to himself and everybody else. Were used to him though; don't pay him no mind at all. If he wants to be contrary, let him. I will say this; he knows his trade, but you just have to take Rufus as he is." With that Julies said, "If it's a boat that you want, there is raft hauling freight, and sometimes passengers. If you're lucky, you might catch it being loading up for a trip now."

Jess thanked them for helping, and didn't tell them his purpose, but replied, "I'm Jess Fulmer. I knew that there had to be a boat or ferry around here somewhere. I'm trying to get to Missouri and just wasn't sure if there was a town nearby."

Julie's wife, Ann, spoke up and asked, "Got folks in Missouri? We got folks out there. They say the lands good but I heared the soil is thin. They are thinking about coming back. I can't say as I blame em though, what with all them Indians movin in there."

Jess didn't comment on the Indians, but said that he just wanted to see what that part of the country was like. The Parkers asked where he had come from, and asked for any news that he might have. Jess didn't divulge much, but did tell them about his family; saying that he just got tired of being by himself, and had decided to look the country over.

After about a short ride, they came into a rather nondescript town. It did have a main street with a saloon or two, a general store, and a black smith shop. There was also a ware house and a loading dock. A large raft was tied up at the dock, and three men were loading goods onto it.

The Parkers said that they had to pick up some things at the general store, and said that they might see him later on. They parked in front of the store, and Jess rode over to the warehouse. He dismounted, tied Sal to a hitching post and walked over to the raft.

He stood watching as the men loaded goods. Jess was amazed at how many things were being loaded on. The vessel had a small cabin in the middle for shelter against bad weather. It even had a small corral for animals.

As Jess watched, one of the men stopped long enough to ask if he wanted passage. He said, "I'm Tim Edwards, I own this raft and I'm organizing a trip down the river. Where you headed?"

Jess replied, "I'm headed for the Shawnee Indian reservation in Missouri."

"Tim said, I don't guess it's any of my business, but why would you want to go to that God forsaken place? Ain't nothin there but misery and starvation. We freighted that flea bitten lot down there a good while back, and they shore didn't have anything going for them. To be honest, I felt real sorry for them, even if they did stir up a ruckus in this country."

Jess replied that he had some business to tend to, and also that he wanted to look the country over. Then Jess asked about the cost of passage.

"Well, now, is it just you and your horse, or do you have luggage?"

"No, luggage; I'm not planning on staying there much more than two weeks. I've got everything I need on my horse."

"Okay, if that's all you are going to bring, perhaps we can work something out. I won't charge you any freight, and I'll provide feed for your horse; if you will hire on to help."

Jess didn't see how he could turn down such an offer, so he agreed to Tim's terms if he was able to do the same thing on the return trip. Then he asked, "How long will it be before you come back?"

Tim stated, "We have to float downriver, unload our cargo, sell the raft, and ride the steam boat back. If everything goes according to plan, I'd say in about three weeks or so. It could be more or less; it all depends. You could go over land, and maybe get back here sooner. But, like I said, it could be three weeks round trip."

Jess, wasn't too sure what to do. He had no idea what he would find in Missouri.
The trip might be wasted. But then, looking over new country might be worth it.

Tim asked Jess if he was ready to get to work. Jess told him to lead on. They went into the warehouse, and Tim directed him to start loading sacks of corn along with bags of salt. It was all a part of the payment that the Government and the Shawnee had agreed to in the treaty. It took most of the day to load the cargo, and they finally finished at dusk.

Tim suggested to Jess that they find some supper, and rest up for the trip the next day, saying, that there was ample room on board, and that the horse could be put in the raft's corral.

Jess and Tim walked to the general store and bought some ham and a loaf of bread for their supper, then went back to the raft and cooked the ham on the raised hearth in the rafts shelter. Soon they were sipping coffee and eating. Jess made him comfortable, and listened to the river lapping against the raft. The slow movement of the river, and the slow undulation of the craft had its effect on him and he began drifting off to sleep.

It was just daylight when Jess awoke. Tim and the other men were loading a few more things on the raft. They hurriedly put everything in its place and made ready to cast off. Jess asked if there was anything he could do to help. Tim said, "Yes, there is, why don't you see what you can do to help George cast the ropes off. We are about ready to head down stream."
Jess complied, and it wasn't very long before the raft began nosing its way out into the middle of the river.

Tim introduced the other workers. They were George Write, and Phil Smith. Soon they began steering the raft well away from snags that protruded out of the water and started drifting down stream.

Sal, who had been corralled, didn't care for the raft at all. When Jess had first put her on board, she had seemingly accepted it and had just looked around and observed the comings and goings of the four men as they loaded the supply's. But now, since they were on the river, she began to pull against her restraint trying to get away from the rolling motion of the craft. Sal snorted loudly, then started kicking and stomping her feet. Jess tried to get her calmed her down, but that didn't stop her nervous behavior. Jess finally walked her around the small corral for a while until she got quiet. As it turned out, Jess had been able to quiet. Jess thought that if Tim decided to land the raft along the way, he could take Sal for a ride to further calm her. But there was no mention of stopping.

As the day progressed towards dusk, Tim lit lanterns on the raft to let any other craft know of their whereabouts. It would never do to have a collision on the river.

It was about Ten o'clock in the evening when Tim said, "Fellows, we can't stay up all night, so why don't you George, and you Phil turn in and I'll roust you out about three am. That way we can all get some rest. If there is any trouble between times, I'll wake you. George and Phil gladly lay down, for working the raft had been an arduous ordeal.

Jess and Tim kept a close eye on the river as best they could, for the lanterns didn't put out much light. fortunately there were no serious mishaps. They did have a close call with a smaller raft, but it pushed away at the last minute.

Tim woke up George and Phil for their shift and reported that all went well. He and Jess turned in until it was their turn to work the raft again. George and Phil guided the raft, and the night passed quietly.

With the sunrise, the wind began to blow causing waves of water to wash over the raft, impeding its progress. The men had to hold on for dear life as the raft pitched and rolled. Jess had to hobble Sal, so she couldn't break free. She began pulling at her harness in an effort to get away from the water washing over the raft, but the hobbles secured her. Sal just hung her head and stood very still. There was nothing Jess could do to help Sal this time. He felt so sorry for her, but went about his chore making sure the cargo was still in place; while Tim worked the rudder and George and Phil manned the poles. The wind blew hard, tossing the raft to and fro, and Tim looked for a place to land, and finally spotted still water along the shoreline. He began inching the vessel close in to the bank. When they had gotten near enough Phil took a rope and secured it to a tree.

The wind was still blowing, but there were signs that it was letting up. The raft was in a safe sheltered place and after about an hour, the wind finally eased up. The men breathed a sigh of relief, and took stock of their cargo. Everything seemed okay, except for some of the ropes that had loosened a little. That was quickly fixed, and then they waited a while before going out on the river again.

Having helped to secure the raft, Jess said that he thought he should see to his horse, and ride her for a while; to make certain she was alright. Jess talked to Sal in quiet tones, and then saddled her. At first she wouldn't budge, but she finally let Jess lead her to the edge of the raft, and then onto the shore. Sal didn't care for the confines of the raft and its unstable motion. The familiar feel of the ground felt very comforting to her, and she pranced around in enjoyment. Jess didn't like putting Sal on the raft but

but there was not much he could do about it. Jess rode her for about a half an hour or so to try and keep her settled down, and then headed back to the raft. At first he couldn't get Sal to go on board. He finally had to coax her with a bucket full of feed.   Jess didn't blame her for not wanting to get back on the raft, but there was no other choice.   When Jess got her back into the corral, Sal turned her back to him and snorted as if she was saying, I'm mad. Jess just laughed and said, "Women.

It took about two weeks for the raft to get to its destination. When it did, Tim went to see the Indian Agent on the reservation. When Tim finally came back, he had brought several Indians to help with the unloading of their cargo.

When the Indians saw Sal, they stopped to admire her, and then they began trying to trade for her, but of course Jess would have none of that. They offered him furs, a gun, and some blankets; all of which Jess turned down. The Indians weren't about to give up on Sal, and started dickering with him again. The Indian Agent finally came to the corral and told them get back to work. Jess thanked him, and the agent said, "If I were you, I'd keep a very close eye on your horse. Those Indians aren't past stealing her." This gave Jess a chance to ask about Grey Wolf. He said, "Sir, my name is Jess Fulmer. I'm from over in Licking County Ohio. Have you got just a moment to spare? I have a question to ask you."

"Sure son, I'll try to answer your question as best I can. By the way, I'm Rex Albertson, the Indian Agent. Now then, what is your question?"

First Jess explained why he was there, and said, "Sir, I feel obligated to Grey Wolf,
and am trying to find him. I know it might not be possible, but I would like to try."

Mister Albertson pause before answering, and then

Replied, "Son, you are a very unusual person. There aren't many that would take the time to help an Indian. Everyone else wants to run them off. Why would you want to help this one Indian?"

Jess asked himself that same question. The only answer he could come up with was that he felt it was his duty. Then he said, "I might never be able to find Grey Wolf, and even if I did, there is no reason to believe that he would want to go back. Even so, it is something I must see through."

"Well now, that is remarkable. Tell you what I'll do. I'm going to ask around, but you do know, that if you find him, the others will try to dissuade him, plus the fact that I may have something to say. Nevertheless, I will ask around. And another thing, I wouldn't go messing around over on the reservation if I were you. As I told you before, those Indians would do almost anything to get your horse!"

Jess wasn't about to go traipsing around on an Indian reservation; unless of course he had a guide with him. But it seemed to Jess that the Lord was working things out through the Indian agent.

After the Indians had unloaded the raft, Mister Albertson and Tim talked for a while. Presently Tim came back and said, "Men, Mister Albertson has agreed to buy the raft from me. They almost always do, but you never can tell. The Government gives the logs to the Indians, and sometimes the Government uses them. I don't care what they do with it, as long as I get my pay.

The Indians had departed by this time, so the men began dismantling the raft. Jess had taken Sal to a group of trees and tied her there, and about an hour later, he glanced over at Sal and saw some Indians looking at her. He didn't go over there, but he did keep an eye on them. The last thing he wanted was to be afoot on an Indian reservation.

When the raft had been taken apart and the logs stacked, Jess asked Tim what they were going to do now. Tim said, "Jess, I think we are going to camp out until the steamboat comes. I don't really know how long it will be until it shows up, but it is pretty regular in its schedule, unless it runs into a snag. You are welcome to camp with us. The steamboat will be here sooner or later." Jess didn't feel like he had a choice so he said that he would stay around until he heard from the Indian agent. If the steamboat came before then, he would just wait and ride his horse back home.

The men made camp in the trees close to Sal, to make the Indians didn't try to steal her, and then they settled in to wait for the steam boat.

A few days later, Rex Albertson had some news for Jess. He said that there was indeed a young buck named Grey Wolf, and he had talked to him, and that he agreed to meet with Jess that very day.

The steamboat hadn't showed up as yet, and so the men just stayed at the camp.

It was late in the afternoon, when Jess saw an Indian petting his horse. At first he didn't recognize who it was. He said, "That horse is not for sale! Get away from here!"

The Indian replied, "I'll give you a big fat chicken for it," and then he started laughing and turned around. It was Grey Wolf, and he extended his hand to Jess and asked, why have you come?

Jess replied, "Shouldn't we seek one another?"

Grey Wolf seemed pleased at this remark and said, "The agent said that someone was looking for me. I had no idea it was you. It is very good to see you. Is everything alright?"

"Yes, everything is good. I have some folks looking after the farm while I am away."

Grey Wolf looked puzzled and asked, "Why are you

here you Jess Is all well?"

Jess didn't say why at first, but said, "Oh, I had a hankering to see some of the country, and just thought I would take a ride."

"Take a ride! That was some ride, but I don't think it was for pleasure. Why did you really come here?"

Jess pondered for a moment, and then said, "Grey Wolf, my parents built our home on land that once belonged to your people. I know that there was a treaty made, but then when you came to live with me, I began to think long and hard about what had happened to you, and it bothered me. The more I thought about it, the more I realized how wrong that was. You have more or less been forced to give up your homes so that we can have them.   The reason I came here was to offer some of your land back.

While riding in the woods, I came across one of your people's old villages. As I looked around I found a necklace made with bear claws. It was in the dirt, and I brought it with me to give to you." Jess went to his saddle bags and produced the necklace.

Grey Wolf took the necklace and looked at it. He held it tightly in his hands, and when he spoke, his voice quavered. Then he said, "Jess, do you know who this belonged to? This was my father's necklace. It had been handed down from his father. I didn't think I would ever see it again. I looked everywhere for it. "Jess was really dumbfounded. He couldn't believe what happened. He said, "Grey Wolf, you know, when I first started this journey, I had my doubts about it, but now I know that it must have been meant to be. You now have your father's necklace, and a place to call home if you want it. I have done what I set out to do, and haven't regrets." Then Jess asked, "Grey Wolf, what do you think? Would you like to come back to your home, or have you broken all ties to that place?"

Grey Wolf hesitated then said, "Jess, that is kind of

you, and I am very grateful, but I have found some of my family. My parents are dead, but there are those here that need me. I don't want to abandon them. Perhaps if things change I will come home.   But, I must stay."   Jess said he understood, and so the two talked about the days gone by and of his people's condition.   Grey Wolf told Jess about the other reservation in Kansas, and some of the Indians were thinking about going there to see what it was like.

Jess inquired about Grey Wolf's welfare, asking how many of his family had survived the removal. As it turned out, many of them did survive, but some had perished in the last winter. There had been a lack of food, and their shelters weren't very warm.

Jess was saddened to hear about this and he sympathized with him saying, "Grey Wolf, that is one of the reasons that I came looking for you. I was concerned for your welfare. But you look as if you are doing well."

Grey Wolf looked at him with a sadness in his eyes and replied,   "Jess, my friend, I am young and strong but many aren't doing that well. The government gives us corn, but we must hunt our food, and the game is getting scarce. That is one of the reasons why we want to go to the reservation in Kansas; to see if conditions are any better out there. It is a hard decision to make, but it must be done; our survival depends on it."

Jess could see that Grey Wolf would never leave his people, and he understood that. He wouldn't want to leave his family either.   Yet he had thought of selling the farm his family had built. The journey he had been on, and seeing firsthand the plight of Grey Wolf's people, had opened up his eyes.   Abigail was waiting for him, and the possibility of having his own family was becoming a reality.   The urge to return home came over Jess as he thought of what could be.

Never again would he take for granted the legacy his family had left him. Unlike the Indians, it wasn't likely that someone was going to try and take his home away. He could see his future rising up while Grey Wolf's future was unsure.

Grey Wolf and Jess continued their conversing, promising to try and keep in touch. Jess told him that if things didn't work out the way he wanted, that his offer still stood and a plot of ground was waiting for him if he wanted it.

After some time, Grey Wolf said that he had better get back to the reservation. The two friends shook hands together and Grey Wolf left; not knowing if they would ever see each other again.

Jess went back to the campfire; for it was getting dark and he began settling down for the night. Tim, George and Phil had been upstream fishing, and they came back with a stringer full of small catfish. While Tim and George cleaned the fish, Jess made coffee and Phil got the frying pan ready.

As the men sat around the fire, a long lonesome sound drifted through the air. It seemed to be quite a way off. It was the distinct sound of the steamboat's horn. Tim stood up and said, "Get ready boys, here comes our ride. It's the steamboat. I told you she would show up. She has a ways to go from the sound of it, but it won't be all that long, before we will be headed home."

Jess began to wonder if he should even try to get Sal onto the steamboat. If he could, it wouldn't take all that long to get back home to see Abigail. But on the other hand, if he did take the boat, he would miss seeing new territory. It was going to be a tossup, and he would just have to wait until morning to see how it would work out. Jess didn't like waiting around for answers, but he had no choice. It would all depend on how Sal acted.

The men sat around the fire speculating as to when the steamboat would arrive. Tim was of the opinion that it would tie up somewhere for the night; because of the snags. If that was the case, it could be late morning before it came. They stayed up, watching the stars until sleep began to overtake them and one by one they went to bed.

Long about three in the morning Jess was startled awake by Sal. He got out of bed just in time to see a dim figure slipping through the trees, but whoever it was, had vanished into the underbrush. It was obvious that an Indian had tried to steal her. He talked to Sal, petting her until she settled down. Jess didn't bother going back to bed, but led Sal closer to the fire, and waited for daylight.

The next day was damp, and there was a low fog hanging over the river. It drifted up around the camp in an undulating motion. The dampness began settling down around the trees, and Tim remarked, "This fog is about as thick as pea soup. The steamboat will be delayed no doubt. I don't see how the boat going to navigate in this stuff."

George replied, "I have no idea what will happen, but this I do know, that old boat will show up.

Phil didn't hesitate to reply, and said, "I saw a steamboat once that come out of a fog bank. It had its horn a blarin away, with thick smoke coming out of its stack. It looked like some kind of river monster a bearin down on me. I almost jumped out of my skin!"

They laughed at Phil's humorous remark, and presently a long loud blast came from the river. After a good while they could hear the steamboat's paddle wheel churning as it made its way down stream.

Every ten minutes, the steamboat would sound its horn to warn anyone on the river to get out of the way. About an hour and a half later the steamboat emerged from the dense fog bank, and stopped close to the shore. The captain of the boat gave one last long blast on the horn, and Sal jumped sideways, trying to get away. Jess went to her and tried to calm her down. It was a good thing he had her tied to a tree, or she would have broken and run. As it was, Jess had quite a time with her. The steamboat did look intimidating as it came out of the fog, sounding its horn. It was no wonder Sal tried to get away.

When the gangplank was finally lowered, several men came down the plank and tied the steamboat to piling's set in the ground to keep the boat from drifting away from the shore. Then some bags of salt, corn and flour were unloaded. Then Rex Albertson showed up with several Indians and then they began loading the commodities. Soon other Indians drifted in to get a look at the steam boat; admiring it for its size, and pointing at the paddlewheel. They were fascinated and tried to go on board, but the captain prevented them. One Indian tried to push his way past the captain of the boat and a scuffle ensued. For a moment it looked as if the captain was going to get pitched overboard and into the river. Rex Albertson quickly ran to his aid and told the Indians to leave. They protested, saying they only wanted to see the big canoe. After a few moments the Indians left.

Mister Albertson said that the Indians were only curious about the boat, and that they wouldn't bother anything at all, but said that it might be better to have one of the men stay on guard just in case.

Jess, had doubts about the steamboat, and getting his horse on board. He wasn't too sure if Sal would go up the gangplank. He thought about using blinders, but wasn't all that sure about it. Sal had already been spooked, and that alone was a strike against loading her. Jess wasn't all that sure he wanted to ride on it himself. He had about all of the river travel that he wanted.

As he was pondering, Grey Wolf suddenly showed up. He asked, "Jess, how much longer are you going to be here? I just wanted to see you once more before you go."

"I'm glad you came Grey Wolf. I was just trying to decide if I wanted to ride in the boat, or to go home horseback. I've just about made up my mind to ride my horse home. I don't trust that steamboat. It's noisy and would probably scare Sal out of her wits. She is already jumpy about it."

"It is an unnatural thing to her, and in her mind, it poses a threat. I would advise riding her home. It could prove to be the shortest route after all."

"You are right. The slow way can be the best way. Besides, I'll get to see more of this country."

The two friends passed time in easy conversation until Tim came over and asked if Jess was going on the boat, saying that he had made arrangements with the captain, if he wanted to go that way. The boat was departing within the hour, so Jess told him that he wanted to ride Sal home, and that he was in no real hurry. Tim thanked him for his help, and wished him good luck, and he, George, and Phil boarded the boat.

As Jess and Grey Wolf stood talking, three Indians came over, and asked to see his horse. Jess said okay but that it wasn't for sale. One of the Indian's said, "I will buy her from you. I will give you another horse and six blankets. I will buy her." The Indians attitude was forceful, but Jess stood his ground proclaiming, "No, and for the last time, my horse is not for sale at any price! I'm getting tired of this. So git!"

The Indian walked over to Sal, and began untying her. "Yes, I am going to buy her. I want her. You will sell her to me now!" Jess shook his head at the Indians stubbornness; he did not want to have a confrontation at this stage of the game. He wasn't one to back down from trouble.

Grey Wolf went to the Indian telling him to leave before something bad happened.

The Indian said, "What are you going to do, stop me from buying this horse?"

Jess had come to Sal's side, saying again, "No, he isn't going to stop you, I am." With that, Jess got the Indian by his hair, bent him backwards, kicked his feet out from under him and let him fall to the ground. The Indian jumped up and tried to grapple with Jess, but he just punched the Indian in the nose and tossed him to the ground. It had happened so fast that the Indians were dumbfounded and did nothing. Then Jess said to him in a firm voice. "This horse is not for sale!" The Indian got up, turned on his heel and left.

Grey Wolf said, "Jess, you have just made an enemy. I admit that he deserved what he got, but just the same, you had better watch your back while you are here."

"Well, I wasn't going to stay much longer anyway. It's high time I went home. I've got to get back and take care of business."

Jess and Grey Wolf lingered a little while longer then Jess saddled Sal. He and Grey Wolf shook hands. Jess said, "My offer still stands. I won't work the land, I want you to have it just in case you change your mind sometime." I will hold it for you. Then Jess mounted his horse. Grey Wolf held up his hand in a salute and watched as Jess rode

Chapter 14

When Jess left the Indian reservation, he started off on a trail that followed the river. The narrow trail led away from the river, on an upward ascent into a mountain. He didn't have much choice but to follow it, because the trail ended at a large swamp. He turned away from the swamp and continued on his way, guiding Sal up through the trees along a twisting path. The higher they went upward, the narrower the path became. Finally, after about an hour of riding, they came out on a bench that was very thick with brush. The trail seemed to have stopped, but as Jess looked around he spotted where it exited the brush and continued on up the mountain. Just as he was about to work his way through the brush, he heard the twang of a bow, and an arrow whizzed past his head. He didn't wait around to see who had shot at him, but prodded Sal, and made for the path on the other side of the brush. Jess had just entered the path when he felt a sudden pang of pain in his right arm. An arrow had nicked him, and he heard the shout of a voice. Jess didn't even slow down, but went plunging up the trail and out of harm's way.

The pain in Jess's arm was getting bad, but he didn't stop, even though the wound needed attending. He continued riding hard for at least a half an hour until deeming it safe to stop. Sal needed a breather any way. Jess had found concealment under some overhanging tree limbs and tended wound.

The arrow had grazed his arm, but the cut was deep enough that it required bandaging. He dressed it as best he could; all the while keeping a close eye on his surroundings.

As near as Jess could tell, he hadn't been followed. he wondered if it was the Indian he had fought with.

After resting a while he mounted Sal and started up the path again, this time going at a much slower pace. The danger seemed to have past, but Jess kept a wary eye out just in case the danger returned.

It was around two in the afternoon when Jess came upon a log cabin nestled among the trees. There didn't seem to be anyone around, but he called out, "Hello the house." There was no answer. Jess dismounted and knocked on the door, but again, there was no response, so he tried the door, and it swung open. Jess felt a little apprehensive about the situation, and cautiously looked inside. The cabin seemed to be abandoned. He stepped through the door and started looking around. There was a small rustic table in the middle of the room with a note on it. It read, Friend, I had to go over the mountain for some grub. I won't be back for a while. Make yourself to home, and leave it as you found it.   Cut me some firewood for pay.   You won't find many fixens, but there is coffee. Just take what you need for your stay. Dan Ralph.

Jess decided that he might as well take advantage of a place to stay, so, he looked around for an ax, and found one in a small shed at the back of the cabin. He located a pile of fire wood and commenced to split and stack it. Each time that Jess swung the ax he winced, but managed to finish his chore. Jess went back inside, built a fire in the fireplace, got his gun, and went hunting for some small game. It wasn't long before he shot a rabbit; he dressed it out and fried the rabbit in the fireplace. His arm was really throbbing, so Jess didn't over work it but lounged around the cabin all day. He had tied Sal to one of the porch posts, and she seemed content.

As the day progressed and the sun began setting. Jess made ready for a good night's rest. He was glad that he hadn't gone on the boat; even after being shot at. The wound was alright, but it was sore from chopping fire wood. Had it been more than a graze, he wouldn't have been able to do it.

As darkness fell, Jess checked on Sal to make sure no one was trying to steal her. His apprehension wasn't uncalled for, because it was an unknown place to him and he wasn't all that sure if there were any Indians.

About ten o'clock, sleep overcame him, and the next thing he knew, it was morning. Jess went outside to check on Sal; she was still there. He untied her, and led her over to a patch of deer grass growing nearby, and then he went to the well in the yard and brought her a drink out of a bucket. He then went back inside, warmed up some left over coffee and also warmed up the remaining rabbit for his breakfast.

Jess gave the cabin the once over to make sure everything was as he found it. Before going out, he reached into his pocket and placed a coin on the table as payment for the night's stay. His arm was still rather sore, but not so sore that he couldn't ride. Then he saddled Sal for the long ride back home. The saddle pleasantly squeaked as Jess mounted up. It was a reassuring sound, and he pulled his hat a just little tighter on his head. The smell of the leather, the coolness of the morning, and just the thought of getting back to see Abigail again, spurred Jess onward down the trail.

Along about nine o'clock, Jess came to a small clearing and stopped to let Sal graze on sparse grass growing there. It wasn't much, but sufficient until he could get grain. The surrounding forest was teaming with wildlife; so Jess stopped to shoot some game. He tethered Sal, and walked a short distance and waited. It wasn't long before he had shot a squirrel or two. Then he mounted up, and continued on his way.

Jess was riding through some very rough terrain, with large overhanging ledges of rock along the trail. He had been riding along in a northeasterly direction trying to get down off of the mountain, making as much time as possible, but his footing too wasn't sure. Jess traveled on until he was forced to stop by a sudden gust wind. Then there was a bright flash of light, and a loud crash of thunder that reverberated through the surrounding hills. Now Jess wished he had stopped less than one of the overhangs a while back, but there was nothing to do but go forward until some kind of shelter could be found.

Jess had gone a few hundred yards when he suddenly came upon another overhang, and he quickly made for it. There was just enough room for Sal; he dismounted and led her underneath the protruding rock. As Jess looked around, he could see where someone else had used the overhang as a temporary shelter before him. There was a good supply of firewood and he saw the ashes of an old campfire. He wondered if it could have been Dan Ralph. Jess got some of the wood and built a fire. The storm raged around him and the lightening continued flashing while the thunder boomed, shaking the ground.

Sal didn't care for the storm, and she nervously pranced about, shaking her head, but and after a few minutes she finally got quiet. Jess removed the saddle and bed roll and that seemed to help.

After Jess had the fire going, he dressed a squirrel and cooked it for his lunch. The storm raged, but he had shelter and something to eat. He was content.

As Jess sat by the warm fire, his thoughts returned to Abigail. He began to wonder if he had made a fool of himself by riding away like he did. Jess thought it over and after a while, knew that given the chance, he would do it again, except, perhaps, getting shot at by an Indian.

He was glad he had gone after Grey Wolf and had been able to present him with the bear claw necklace. It seemed strange that it had belonged to his father. It was as though providence had sent him on an errand.

The more he thought about his journey, the more he began to realize that the hand of God had been in it from the first.

Jess and Sal waited out the storm; while the fire crackled and shadows danced around the shelter. He stretched his hands to the warmth of the fire, relaxing in its glow.

The next day, Jess continued riding up the trail until it divided. One path went on up the mountainside while the other one descended down into the valley. He paused for a while trying figure out which way would be best. As he sat there, Sal became alert. Jess reached for his gun, and in a moment, he saw a man riding a horse and leading a pack mule up the trail. When the man got close, Jess spoke to him and said, "Sir, you have quite a load."

"Stranger, I thought someone might be up here. My horse told me that. Where might you have come from?"

"Well, I came from the Indian reservation and I'm headed back home to Ohio."

"Ohio? What in tarnation made you come here?

Let's just say I was I errand of mercy."
The man said,'m Dan Ralph. Who, you might be?"

"I'm Jess Fulmer, and while we are at it, I want to thank you for letting me stay in your cabin. It was a God send. I had been shot at by an Indian, and had to clean up my wound. I really needed the rest."

"Good thing them Indians are by the river, they can Be a heap of trouble if they've a mind to."

Jess didn't even mention Grey Wolf, but steered the conversation in another direction. He said, Sir, I'm trying to decide the quickest way to the Ohio River. You are the first person I've seen since I stayed in your cabin. I'm afraid I might get lost up here, and I have no desire to back track."

Dan Ralph looked at Jess and said, "Son, you don't have to call me Sir, just call me Dan. If you want to get home in a week or two, I'd follow the trail I just came up on. It will take to take you down to the village of Breakwater. When you get there, just follow the River Road to the east. The terrain will change some, but you want to stay down in the valley. You will be able to ferry across the river over onto the Ohio side. It's a long ride, but I'd rather ride a horse than a boat, if, you had a mind to look the country over.

Jess agreed with him and replied, "Dan, I could have ridden the steamboat, but it made my horse nervous. She was acting up when that steamboat blew its whistle. I couldn't see any sense in scaring her to death. This horse is my friend and I just couldn't put her through any more strain than she has already had. I know we have a long ride ahead of us, but we are up to it."

"You have a good lookin mare. What's her name?"

Jess replied, "Her name is Sally, but I like to call her Sal."

Dan busted out laughing and replied, "Not Sally! Why, I knew an old gal named Sally. She could outride anyone, and played a getar to boot. She was a sight to behold." Dan laughed and said, "I'd much rather look at your Sal as to look at her. She was as ugly as an old mud fence, and had the personality of a cactus. I doubt if that old gal ever got hitched. Who'd want a prickly oldwoman like her?"

Dan laughed again and said that time was waistin, and he had better git to the house. Then he repeated his instructions and told Jess to keep an eye out for the moonshiners, saying that they weren't all that bad, but if they just happened to need a horse, they aren't past borrowing without asking. Jess watched as Dan headed up the mountain.

Jess didn't turn onto the trail going down the mountainside right away, but sat still and watched Dan until he disappeared around a bend. He was glad to have met him. It wasn't everyone who would let a stranger use their cabin and their coffee.

Jess sat for a little while longer pondering upon the folks he had met on his journey. So far everything had gone just fine, except for the encounter with the Indian who had shot at him. It could have been much worse, but God had kept him safe thus far, and trusted that he would be guided home in safety.

The trail down into the valley was steep, and Jess had to lean back in the saddle to keep from sliding forward. Sal took her time, and was careful where she stepped. Jess helped guide her around boulders in the trail, and at times they had to squeeze through brush and saplings growing close to the trail. It was slow going at times, but they did make steady progress.

It was along about noon, when they came upon small stream that crossed the trail. Jess dismounted and filled his canteen and let Sal get a drink. There were signs that someone had recently crossed. He studied the tracks, and it was obvious to him that it had been Dan because there were two sets of tracks in the mud. There were also other tracks that led upstream into the woods. The only thing he could think was that they were the moonshiners. Jess mounted Sal and crossed the stream and continued on. As they wound their way along the trail, they came to a rather deep ravine. The trail went down one steep side and up the other. Jess urged Sal to start on down it. She took her time, choosing her footing. But when they came out at the bottom, she didn't wait for

Jess to nudge her, but lunged forward and raced up the hill and into the trees beyond. Jess sat straight in the saddle and hung on to the saddle horn to keep from being thrown off. It was a thrilling ride, and Sal had performed perfectly. Jess didn't stop, but rode on up the trail making good time. He wanted to find a place to camp out before nightfall, because there more miles of riding ahead. The terrain was rather rough in places and he didn't want to wear Sal out; so he looked for a good place for the night. Jess rode on for about two hours, until coming upon a small patch of deer grass beside a pool of water. Jess dismounted, tethered Sal and started making camp; setting up his tent a short distance from the water. He noticed that the spot had been used, because there was evidence that a fire had been built not all that long ago. The ashes were quite cold; so it must have been a day or two before. He settled in, and then began gathering firewood, and settled in.

Jess remembered the moonshiners and tethered Sal next to the tent. He didn't want to be left afoot in the mountains. He hoped that Sal would warn him of any danger, but he wasn't taking chances.

Long about nightfall, Sal began stamping her feet, and started looking in the direction of the trail. Jess went to her side and tried to see what had disturbed her. A large bobcat came slinking along. When it got abreast of them, it paused and emitted a low growl. Sal tried to back away from this menace but the tether held her tight. Jess picked up a stick and hurled it at the bobcat but it sidestepped the stick and hurried on its way. Sal snorted loudly as if to say, and don't come back. She then settled down, and started nibbling on some dried weeds.

The next morning, Jess awoke to find that there were more storm clouds gathering. He quickly stirred the embers of the fire and made coffee.

He had run short of his food, and must now replenish it as best he could. There was a good chance that he would get into Breakwater sometime that day, and he would be able to restock his food supply. Jess got his rifle and took to the woods to try and find breakfast.

When Jess got back to camp, he built the fire up, cleaned the rabbit he had shot and began cooking. Jess had just finished when a gust of wind came, and with it, a few drops of rain. Fortunately he hadn't taken the tent down, so Jess grabbed the coffee pot and his breakfast and went into the tent to wait for the rain to come. He began to wonder if all it did was rain in that part of the country.

Jess drank the coffee, ate the rabbit and watched as the wind began blowing leaves and debris all around the camp. Presently the aroma of dampness filled the air.

When the rain finally came, it thundered down in torrents, and was whipped around by the wind, and then a lightning bolt struck a tree close to camp.
It came crashing down in splinters. Jess jumped at the report of thunder, and wished that the storm would pass them by.

The storm, seemed anchored to the area, and the sea of clouds grew darker with each passing moment. Then it stopped raining and a great hush fell on the landscape. Jess could feel a tenseness filling the atmosphere and he got apprehensive. The quietness became frightening. After a few moments, the wind suddenly picked up. The clouds started to swirl around and around forming a dark vortex, and slowly began lowering to the ground. A great roaring sound started. Jess could feel pressure mounting, it made his ears pop. Suddenly the wind whipped around the camp almost tearing the tent from its stakes. Jess held onto it as best he could and waited out the storm

Trees further into the woods were being tossed around like so many matchsticks, and then, as suddenly as it came, the storm abated; the clouds being driven before the force of the wind.

Jess gave a sigh of relief and began to take stock of his belongings. Everything was intact in the tent, but the ground around the tent was littered with tree limbs and leaves. Sal was okay, and it seemed a miracle that they hadn't been hurt. God had evidently been watching over them. His eye was indeed on the sparrows Jess thought. It had been a close call indeed.

Chapter 15

"Breakwater, Missouri," Population 102. Jess wasn't impressed. He thought this town might be a little bit bigger. He didn't really know why he thought that it would be bigger. Perhaps it was because of the conversation with Dan Ralph. Or maybe he was ready to get home and see Abigail again. It seemed ages since he last saw her. Jess visualized their meeting in the kitchen when he kissed her good bye. It spurred him on. Jess had deliberately avoided thinking of Abigail. He had been preoccupied with his journey to find Grey Wolf, and also with the storms on the mountain, but that was behind him, and now, Jess was looking forward to the journey home to her.

When Jess rode down the muddy main street of Breakwater, he began looking around for a supply store and soon found one in the town square. It was next to a saloon and loud piano music came spilling out onto the street. Jess just shook his head and went into the supply store. One of the first things he saw was a cracker barrel. He hadn't had a cracker since no telling when. He looked inside the barrel and got one; they were still good, so he decided to buy some for the trip home.

"Howdy," someone said. An older woman came out from the back of the store. She wore a gingham dress, and had her gray hair done up in a bun on top of her head. She seemed pleasant so Jess answered, "How do, I came in to get a few things, and be on my way again."

"What brings you to Breakwater?"

"Oh, I've been at the Indian reservation on some business, and I'm returning home."

"You went to an Indian reservation? Well, glory be, I'll bet that place was a sight to see. Them Indians got plum run off of their land. Ain't no wonder they fought us like they did, but I don't hold to their scalpin folks though; it is one thing to fight for what is yours, but some of the things they did was uncalled for. Course, I'm sure we didn't do much better."

Jess wasn't surprised by her remarks, so he steered the conversation to supplies, by saying, "Yes, none of that should ever have happened. By the way, Mam, I'm going to need some things to last me till I get back home. Have you got a slab of bacon? And I'd like a small sack of those crackers and maybe a loaf of fresh- baked bread if you have any. I haven't had fresh bread in a while."

"You are in luck. I bake the best bread you ever had. It goes straight out the door just about as fast as it's baked. I also bake corn dodgers. They will last longer out on the trail. You might want to get some of those, and if you see anything else you need, just let me know."

Jess told her to give him a dozen of the corn dodgers, two pounds of bacon and a loaf of her bread. While she was getting his order together, he looked around for some feed for Sal, and found it off to one side in a wooden bin. He put a sack on a pair of scales next to the bin, and weighed out twenty five pounds of feed and said," Mam," I'm getting twenty five pounds of feed for my horse."

"That's just fine son, I'll add it to the list. Is there be anything else?"

"No, I don't think so. That should get me home alright. I can always hunt if I run out of food. That's what I've done so far. It's my horse I'm worried about. So far she has done okay feeding on wild grass. As long as I come to a town, or a farm, I can get her some feed."

"Whereabouts are you from?" She asked.

Jess didn't hesitate for he knew that folks didn't get

all that much news and he didn't mind sharing with her. He replied, "I'm from Licking county Ohio."
"Well, that sounds like a fer piece."

"Mam, I had a family, but the sickness got them. It got my mom, dad, my sister and brother. I'm alone on the farm."

"Son I'm so very sorry to hear about your loss. But we all go through it sooner or later. You would think a person would get over it in time, but you never do. My husband, Jim, died two years ago; worked himself to death. I surely do miss him, but life must go on. The folks around here rallied around me. I don't have any children, so the little children in this town have become my own. I'm a whole lot like you, I started to pack up and leave this old town; the loneliness was that bad, but the town folks would have none of that."

"I'm glad that you found the fortitude to stay on mam. Much the same thing happened to me. The folks back home looked in on me, and now there is someone special waiting for me when I return."

"Good for you, son, don't be afraid to start a new life. You just take up where your folks left off."

Jess thanked her for the good advice, and started to pay for the supplies, she stopped him. "Wait just a minute son. The whole time we talked, I never even introduced myself. I'm Mary Ann Parker, and I'm glad we met. It isn't often I get to talk to someone that isn't from here. I want to give you my address, and when you get home, and find the time, write me and let me know how things are going. Fill me in if you ever get married. I'd like to know how your story turns out, and, I'm going to give you a jar of my strawberry preserves as a gift."

Jess was very pleased, and replied, "Mary Ann, I'll do as you ask. If everything turns out, I'll be sure and let you know." Then Jess walked out of the store.

Jess had put the supplies on Sal, when someone from the saloon came out on the sidewalk. It was a saloon girl. She looked at Jess and smiled. Her face was painted up and she had bright red lipstick on. She looked like a floozy. Jess turned his head, pretending he hadn't seen her. He tightened the cinch on his horse, and looked everything over one last time before getting into the saddle.

The saloon girl cleared her throat, walked over to Jess and said. "Hey there, Cowboy, why don't you buy me a drink? Its real nice inside and you look a little lonely."

Jess stopped what he was doing and then replied, "Tell you what. Go get some decent clothes on, wash that muck off of your face, and I'll take you to church on Sunday."

The woman laughed and said, "Boy, you are a live one."

"That's right mam, and I plan on keeping it that way." With that, Jess saddled up and rode away, leaving the woman standing there with a dumb look on her face.

Jess headed out, following the river road. He had to laugh at what had just transpired. What fools people can be, he thought. There are all kinds of traps set for a man. It might be someone trying to rob you, or it might be a person like the painted saloon girl, trying to take your soul away. You always have to be on your guard.

The road twisted around the countryside, following the course of the river. Jess rode until midafternoon and stopped to let Sal eat some of the grain he had purchased. It wasn't time to set up camp just yet, and so after eating some bread and jam he started again, putting in as many miles as possible.

About an hour before nightfall came, Jess picked out a place off the road among some oaks and set up camp in a shallow ravine that would hide his fire. There was a small pool of water, and this is where he tethered Sal.

It was just about dark, and Jess had cooked some bacon, and was sipping his coffee when he heard a rider coming down the road. He didn't know if whoever it was would spot the fire, but if they did, they did. Presently the rider came abreast of his camp and stopped. After a few minutes, the person turned the horse towards the trees and advanced a few yards and stopped again. A man called out." Hello the camp. Got any coffee on for a poor traveler?" Jess thought he recognized the voice and replied, "Come on in, it's still hot." The man advanced through the trees and came up to the campfire. When he saw Jess he said, "Well, I'll be jigged!"

Jess laughed and replied, "I'll bet that you never thought you would run into the likes of me out here. How ya doin Bill? It's been a coon's age since you stopped at my place. Get down off your horse and I'll pour you a cup of coffee and fry up some bacon for ya."

Bill Rolland got off of his horse and sat by the fire. "Jess, how ya been doin? I sure didn't think I would run into you. What have you been up to lately?"

Jess told him about his journey, but didn't go into a lot of detail. He said, "Bill, I felt like it was a thing that must be done. Now I'm heading back home; that is where I belong.

Bill remarked, "Jess I have been an old rolling stone most of my life. Many is the time that I wished I had a place to hang my hat, but I just can't get the wanderlust out of my heart. There is absolutely no telling where I'll end up. I'll probably be found out on the dusty plains somewhere. You should be glad that you have a home to go to. There ain't much comfort in being alone."

Jess felt a little bit sorry for Bill, but he didn't say much, except, "Bill, you know where I live. You are welcome at my place anytime. Don't feel like you are intruding; Just come on."

Bill was touched by the gesture, and said, "Why, thank you Jess, but I'm not finished roaming yet. I still got a few years in my hide, and there are some places I really want to see before my time is up. But, I will promise you this. When I do come your way again, I'll take up your offer and stay until the itch hits to climb back into the saddle."

They talked until darkness fell, and when the fire began to die down, Jess put some more wood on, and the two conversed until the stars came out, and then they turned in for the night.

The next morning, Jess got up to find the fire going and the coffee on. Bill was sitting by the fire, and he remarked, "Hey Cowpoke, do you always sleep this late in the day?"

Jess laughed at the remark, and replied. "Not often. Thanks for making the coffee; I'll cook some breakfast. He got the skillet and cut up some bacon in it, then got the loaf of bread, cut it into slices and poured a cup of coffee. Bill saddled up; commenting, "Jess I've sure enjoyed your company, but I got to ride after breakfast."

"Yes, me too Bill, I have quite a long way to go as yet. What direction are you going in? Maybe we can ride together a ways."

"Well, to be honest, I kinda wanted to see New Mexico. I been there once, but that was a long time ago. I might look for work on a ranch out that way. Shoot, you never know, I might end up in Arizona. It all depends on the mood I'm in at the time. I ain't nothing but a tumble weed, without a home."

"Bill, I don't think I could ever keep up with you on the trail." He shook his head and just smiled.

After breakfast, Jess broke camp, put the fire out and loaded Sal. He and Bill talked for a while longer, then saddled up, and parted, with Jess going to the east and Bill going to the south west.

Jess had been glad for Bill's company, and was a little sad to see him go. There was no telling if he would ever see him again. That is the way of life, but each man has to choose his own path. The end result is a person's own doing and they must live with it.

Jess followed the river road all day long until he came to a river crossing. There was a very swarthy looking man with a long black beard attending a raft in the shallows. The river wasn't very wide at this point and there was a rope attached to trees on both sides of the river. Jess inquired as to how much it cost to cross, and if there was a town on the other side.

The man replied, "If it's just you and the horse, it will cost you four bits. As for a town, I wouldn't call it a real town, but more of a restin place. There is a town about five miles farther up the river if you've a mind to go that way. If not, then there is a town about twenty miles downriver."

"Well, sir," I'm going upriver. I have quite a ways to go yet, and I'm going to have to cross the river sometime. I think that this crossing will do." Jess paid the four bits, got Sal onto the raft and watched as the man guided the raft out into the river and on the other side. The crossing was without any incidents, except that Sal was a little nervous, but Jess stood by her, keeping her calm. Before they knew it, they were on the other side of the river on solid ground again. After looking around, Jess understood why the man had said it was a resting place. There was abandoned camps and trash strewn about. Jess followed the river until he had to turn north.

Jess had ridden three weeks; enduring storms, and at times people. He was cautious around people.

The storms could be dealt with, but some folks could not be trusted. Once or twice on the Ohio side, Jess had been followed, but he had hid in the woods, and out foxed them. No doubt he was a target of robbers that were trying to take advantage of what they thought would be an easy target. A man traveling alone had to be on guard at all times.

The closer Jess got to home, the more he thought about Abigail. He couldn't wait to see her again. It seemed like a lifetime since he had left the farm, and now his anxiousness was rising.

It was around ten in the morning, when Jess came upon a cabin among some trees. He stopped and was trying to decide if he should ask for directions when a man came from an outbuilding and hailed him. Jess rode up, and the man spoke to him saying, "You don't look like you are from around here. I don't recognize that horse of yours either. I know most folks in these parts. Whereabouts are you from?"

Jess wasn't at all surprised by the man's approach. He had gotten used to forwardness by this time. He just smiled and introduced himself, "I'm Jess Fulmer from Licking County and I'm working my way back home."

"Where ya bin? Ifin you don't mind my askin."

"Oh, I've just been visiting a friend down south that I haven't seen in a while."

"Down south ya say? It's always good to get to see friends. There was a time when I used to saddle up and head out exploring the country, but my bones won't let me do that anymore. Won't ya lite down fora spell?"

"I'd surely like to, but I've got some miles to go. I want to get as far along today as I possibly can. Do you happen to know how far Licking County is?"

"Oh, I ain't been up that a-way in years, but if memory serves me right, you should get home by the day after tomorrow if you make good time, and don't stop to visit with nosy old men along the way."

The man laughed at his own joke, and Jess couldn't help but join in.

"Sir, Jess said, "it has been a pleasure talking with you today. I needed to visit with someone for a little while. It kind of takes the edge off of my worries. I would stay, but my mind is set on getting home."

"That's alright son, I'd be wantin to get home if I had a gal waitin on me too." The man winked as he made this last remark, and then asked. "Why else would you be in such a hurry? Son you had better git goin. She's a watin on ya."

The next two days were almost an agony to Jess. The last miles of the journey seemed like an eternity. He didn't think he would ever get back home. Even Sal seemed moody and anxious to get home.

The day that Jess expected to arrive, he stopped at a small town to rest for a little while. He was riding in the middle of the main street, when a ruckus erupted down an alley. Someone started shooting at someone else, and before Jess knew what had happened, a stray bullet knocked the hat off his head. Sal started bucking, and then she lunged forward trying to get away from the danger. Jess held on for all his worth, as Sal made a mad dash to the other side of town and out of danger. Jess let Sal have her head until they were a long way from the town.

When Sal finally quit running, Jess got off and took stock of her, and to see if he had lost anything besides his hat, but everything seemed to be in place. Jess hated losing the hat, but he wasn't about to go back. He could replace the hat, but not his life. Jess let Sal catch her breath and found her water to drink, and then let her rest for a while. She had done a good job of getting them away from the danger, and had more than earned the rest.

An hour later Jess was back in the saddle and headed home. His path was now directly north, and soon, he began to see a lot more open fields. Many trees had been thinned out for planting, and by the end of the day, he recognized the terrain.

It was getting rather late when he decided to camp out one more time before making the last push home. He found a likely place with plenty of firewood and a water source. It didn't take long to settle in, and before he knew what had happened, he fell asleep.

When Jess woke up, the sun had already risen, and he got out of the tent and looked around. He couldn't believe he had slept so late.   All of the hard riding had finally gotten to him. Even Sal hadn't moved much. Jess untied her, and let her drink her fill of water while he started a fire to cook on.

It was about eight o'clock when Jess decided that he and Sal were rested enough. They rode until Jess turned onto the road that went past the Springer's house. There was still a ways to go, but that was nothing compared to the miles that were way behind them. Jess was anxious to get on with it, but he didn't want to injure Sal, so he took his time and pondered upon what he was going to say to Abigail when he finally saw her. He thought about stopping to see her, but it was only a few miles to home, so he decided not to stop at the Springers.

It was just about dark when Jess finally got home. He noticed that there weren't any lights in the house. He took Sal to the barn, turned her into a stall. Jess went up to the house, opened the door and stepped in. It looked like the Wilsons had moved out. There was a note on the table. It said, "Jess, thank you for taking us in. Our folks found us, and we decided to go on back East with them. Hope you find everything in place. God bless, and we wish you all the best. Jess wasn't at all surprised by this, the Wilsons wouldn't be around forever. In fact he was pleased that they were gone. They were good people, but he needed his own space.

Jess built up a fire, and then sat down to relax. The next thing he knew he was asleep, and didn't get up until daylight. Jess squinted at the bright sun light, and said, "Oh, man, am I ever glad to be home. I don't think I will ever leave." He got up, and went to the well for a pail of water and washed his face. Then Jess checked on the animals. From what he could see, it looked as if someone had been looking after them, because there was water and feed in place. Jess milked the Jersey cow, then gathered the eggs, and scattered chicken feed around. Jess was pleased. The Wilsons and the Springers had taken care of the farm. He went back into the house, and looked around again. There wasn't a thing out of place. Ruth and Samuel had cleaned the house from top to bottom. He read the note again, and was touched by its sincerity. The Wilsons had really been a Godsend, and he had been a blessing to them. "God sure has a way of working things out," he thought.

Jess was just fixing his breakfast, when he heard a horse coming down the lane. He looked out of the window and saw that it was Caleb Springer. He went out onto the porch, and said, "Well, if it isn't Caleb Springer, my hired hand."

Caleb laughed and replied, "Hired hand?

Jess replied, "I am in great debt to your family. I don't know how I'm ever going to repay what I owe!"

Caleb got off of his horse, and he and Jess went inside.

"Caleb, when did the Wilsons leave out?"

"Oh, the Wilsons left two weeks ago. They did a good job of looking after things. Those were the most grateful folks I have ever met. Their parents got here and they decided to go back east to be closer to their family. I don't blame them. Starting from scratch can be a hard life. Not everyone is cut out for it."

Then Jess asked, "Say, Caleb, how is the family? Is everyone doing well?"

Caleb him-hawed around for a moment or two before answering. He knew who Jess was really asking about, so he purposely delayed answering. Then he replied, "Oh, I guess they are okay." He could tell Jess was anxious to hear about Abigail, so He let him wait for a moment or two longer then smiled and said, "Abigail is just fine Jess. All she talks about is you. I don't think she knows anything else."

"Does it show that bad? I must be making a fool of myself."

"No, Jess, you aren't. But I will say this. I just hope you don't start bleating like some lovesick sheep!" Caleb burst out laughing at his joke, and Jess had to laugh with him.

Jess thanked Caleb for taking care of the farm after the Wilsons left, saying, "I was going to stop over by your place yesterday evening but I was bone tired. I'm going to work around here this morning, and then I'll come over and thank your folks. Tell Abigail hi for me, and that I'll see her after a while."

Caleb mounted his horse and said, "Jess, I'm glad you made it back in one piece. To be honest with you, we were a little bit worried. My mom fretted and worried the whole time. Abigail wasn't any better. Dad had to really talk to her, but now that you are back, they will settle down. I'll talk to you later."

Jess went to the house, and finished preparing his breakfast. He was glad to be home again, under his own roof. Camping out all the time was okay once in a while, but not every day. He was also thankful that God had kept him safe on his journey. There were times that things got kind of dangerous, but I made it.

After Jess made sure that everything was in place

around the farm, he saddled Sal one more time and headed up the lane. As Jess rode along, he couldn't help but wonder at the majesty of God's creation and how that humanity fit into his plan. It was a wonderful thing to ponder upon. The loneliness that had once dominated his life had at last diminished. He could see complete happiness and companionship close upon the horizon. Many things transpired in the last year, and Jess was looking forward to a future with Abigail. He hadn't asked her to marry him as yet, but he felt confident that she would say yes.

When Jess rode up to the Springer's cabin, he dismounted, walked up onto the porch and knocked. Charles Springer opened the door and said, "Well, if it isn't Jess, come home at last. How was the trip son? Glad you made it back safe and sound. The women folk worried about you, but I told them that you were very smart and wouldn't take any chances. It seems that I was right. Come on in here and make yourself at home."

Jess stepped into the house, and made his way to the table and sat down. A moment later, Marta walked into the room. Jess stood up, and she gave him a big hug, and then she said, "Jess Fulmer, you do know that I should scold you for staying away so long, but I won't do it. We are so glad to have you back."

"Oh, Marta, I couldn't help being gone so long. Do you know how far it is to Missouri? I didn't think I would ever get tired of riding and camping, but I sure did, and then I had to ride back; but I made it."

Presently Matthew came in. "I thought that was your horse Jess. Did you have a good time?"

"I did Matthew. I'll tell you all about it sometime."

Just then Abigail walked into the room. She had been fixing her hair, and had used the hair comb in to impress Jess. She looked radiant. He couldn't believe how lucky he was to have such a beautiful woman like

Abigail. His heart raced as he looked into her eyes.

Marta said, "Charles, Mathew, I could use a little help outside, do you mind?" They took the hint, and went outside and let Abigail and Jess have some time alone. Abigail looked at Jess and said, "Jess, I was so worried that something might happen to you! I prayed for you each and every day, and believed that God would bring you home to me." Her face was flushed with emotion, and Jess couldn't help but draw her into his arms. As he held her, he softly replied, "Abigail, there were times that I had to put you out of my mind to keep from turning around and coming back. Now all of that is behind me, and I won't ever leave again. God has healed me of my loneliness and given me a promising future. To be able to stand here with you in my arms is like having a dream come true." As he tenderly kissed Abigail, Jess knew that his journey had ended and he had finally come home.

www.ingramcontent.com/pod-product-compliance
Lightning Source LLC
Chambersburg PA
CBHW050843180626
46814CB00007B/2602